The White Light Meets the Thin Blue Line

A Spiritualist Medium Inside the LAPD

By **Russell Chan**
Serial No. N1735

Preface

A Prayer

May Infinite Intelligence,
Our Guides,
Our Angels,
Our Ancestors and Spirit Friends who love us unconditionally...
May they guide this book into the lives
Of those who need it the most.

So Be It.

Jim: "With your successful readings amongst your LAPD coworkers, you ought to write a book."

Me: "Um...OK."

Joke:

Q: What do you call a short clairvoyant who escaped from prison?

A: A small medium at large.

Most of the names in this book have been changed, especially those of the sitters (message recipients), to protect confidentiality. I treat private mediumship sittings and psychic consultations like a therapy session, unless the sitter is OK with revealing their name. If the mediumship is done on the platform, it is considered to be public.

Journal entries may have been slightly altered to make it more understandable to non-police employees, especially when using department jargon. Some entries were also shortened for the sake of brevity and immediate relevance.

In the tradition of the National Spiritualist Association of Churches (NSAC) and the Morris Pratt Institute (MPI), the title "Reverend" is only used in front of the person's first AND last name. So, you may be wondering why in my book "Reverend Jonathan Doe" is never mentioned as "Reverend Doe" or "Reverend John." I can still type "John Doe," "Jonathan Doe," or "Johnny," but the entire name must appear after the word "Reverend."

Contents

Prologue

There she was, standing in front of me, while I took my break in the courtyard of Police Headquarters Facility, in the heart of downtown Los Angeles.

She was a spirit belonging to the Detective Supervisor who worked on the 9th floor. I just knew it because the spirit looked almost identical to her living loved one. The woman in spirit had the same porcelain-white skin with a hint of freckles, slender build, but with darker hair than the supervisor. She wanted me to convey a message to the Detective Supervisor.

But, I was a budding medium still partly inside the "broom closet" and I was working for the Office of the Chief of Police (OCOP). If I was completely inaccurate about my mediumship skills, the word could get out that there's a delusional "nut job" working right under the Police Chief's nose.

Never mind the Employee of the Quarter award from Foothill Division, Civilian Employee of the Year while at Operations, and the other string of commendations in my personnel folder. If I was wrong about this, my career and reputation could be ruined. Maybe not an offense enough to get fired, but certainly enough to be transferred to some boring basement job, supervised primarily by civilians who love to overcompensate by micromanaging more than the sworn supervisors do. Since the sworn staff ("sworn" meaning "cops," sergeants, lieutenants, etc.) are more trained towards responding to emergencies, they tend to be less petty when it comes to civilian managers. And I don't want to be demoted to "petty."

But, my mediumship training told me that if a message needs to be delivered, as a Spiritualist Medium, you need to do it. You would still have to get permission from the sitter (the message's recipient). That's half the fun.

The spirits trust you to deliver their messages accurately to their living loved ones. If they cannot trust you as a reliable messenger, they can withdraw because word will get around in The Afterlife that you are impossible to work with. It's like being in any organization with a lot of gossip (and cops do like to gossip). If word gets around that someone cannot deliver, that reputation can haunt a person (pun intended) — and that's for the living!

I took notes from the spirit, then went back upstairs to my office on the 10th floor, said a prayer, opened my email and began to type to the Detective Supervisor, risking everything...

Introduction

My department's ID card says "Russell Chan" and my serial number is, and always will be, N1735, even after my physical death. In the Los Angeles Police Department (LAPD), all employees are assigned a serial number. It is always 5-digits. It's always theirs, whether they retire, resign, get fired, or die on or off duty...the serial number is never recycled.

Sworn employees (those that carry guns and badges with the power to arrest people) only get serial numbers that are all numbers. The civilian employees (administrative support, jailers, custodial staff, dispatchers, Department vehicle and helicopter mechanics, etc.) have serial numbers that start with a letter first, followed by 4 numbers. In the Department, we always identify ourselves with our serial numbers, both on documents and sometimes over the phone if both parties don't actually know each other.

During my employment with the City of Los Angeles, I spent my last 23 years with the LAPD, working in two different police stations (Foothill and Mission Divisions), in police human resources (Personnel Division), in Office of Operations, in the Chief of Police's scheduling and admin office, and finally in COMPSTAT Division before retiring and leaving California.

It was in early 2017, while working in Office of Operations (the office which runs about 80% of the Department), that the reason for this book came into being. I felt that I had an unofficial responsibility in bridging the gap between the "free-spirited" world of metaphysics and psychic mediumship, with the skeptical, compartmentalized, no-nonsense world of law enforcement.

At first I thought that my years in law enforcement had nothing to do with learning mediumship until it was pointed out to me that parts of my job did, in fact, prepare me.

First was the gathering of specific details from the victims, the witnesses, and the suspects. Working in Records meant continually inputting people's jobs/careers, driver license numbers, birth dates, addresses, phone numbers, height, weight, hair and eye colors, body markings and alterations, monikers, vehicle description, license plate numbers, descriptions of properties stolen or affected, and the relationships (if any) between the victims and the suspects.

When I first saw a blank mediumship affidavit in the back of my church available for congregants to fill out as a testimonial to the accuracy and authenticity of the medium, I smiled to myself that these details were almost the same things asked for on the front page of an Investigative Report. Instead of the information being tied to a negative event, the details were provided in a way to help identify a spirit, along with objects (like vehicles, heirlooms, houses, etc.) that were unique to the dead or unique to the relationship between the dead and the living.

Some mediums don't prefer the long list of details similar to a police interrogation because they feel that a dead person wouldn't want to be remembered by just their stats, but by the emotions and good times they shared with their loved ones when alive. While I tend to prefer the boring yet detailed descriptors so that I can nail down exactly who is coming through, a sense of compassion will indeed help the medium paint a better picture of the deceased. The second point which prepared me was learning how to have compassion and empathy while still being able to compartmentalize my emotions so that a reading would not overwhelm me emotionally.

After reading hundreds of reports, it is easy to become very detached and look at the reports like one is reading scary fiction. But, even as a civilian hidden away inside an office, we have brief contact with real people involved in these reports. A healthy balance between empathy and detachment helped me not only with my job, but also while on platform giving public readings. Embarking on any such spiritual path, I eventually realized that this responsibility of bridging these two worlds was really bringing together these two aspects within my own personality, first. Perhaps later, it could be accomplished in the outer world.

CHAPTER ONE

Who, ME?

I never knew I was a medium. I figured it was a rare gift that certainly did not belong to me. Sure, I grew up with some psychic and intuitive phenomena and discovered that some family members back in Singapore and other parts of Asia, also had unusual experiences. But deliberate contact with spirits? Nah...

The difference between psychic abilities and mediumship are a little blurry, but still distinct. Being psychic to me was strong intuition. The information I received from people (which I noticed grew strong at the beginning of high school) was just from being around them or thinking of them. Mediumship, however, was getting information from the Dead, either about when they were alive, or information about their living loved ones.

I had the first one, but was only vaguely curious about the second one.

I pretty much kept to myself about the "woo-woo" stuff, only sharing with my best friends, because it is believed that those who have some psychic abilities will attract to themselves people of like mind. I believe this was true because it happened before we had computers and smart phones, and my closest friends had similar experiences and abilities. Before we had computers to bring us together, we relied on Spirit and the psychic version of internal tracking devices. It was like the Universe would draw us together into meeting each other, but we didn't have GPS locators and social apps.

In 1893, the National Spiritualist Association of Churches (NSAC) was formed. Back then, it was called the NSA. Spiritualist churches around the world not only believe in mediums, they include mediums giving messages to the congregation as part of their church's sacrament. You don't have to be a working medium to be a member of a Spiritualist church, anymore than you have to be a monk or nun to be a member of the Catholic Church. That being said, if people are interested in developing their psychic and mediumship abilities, many churches have development circles and training séances, some of which are done in person, and many are done online. These churches also encourage the training and certification of mediums in hopes that these mediums can "serve the platform" (give readings to the public while standing on a platform) at the churches.

My personal interest in how to do mediumship was the practice of mental mediumship in a regular waking state. "Mental mediumship" is when the medium receives information from spirits that no one else can pick up, then the medium relays that information to the living. When it happens, the medium is generally wide awake and in control.

I had no interest in trance mediumship because I like to be in control. "Trance mediumship" is when the medium goes into a trance and the spirit takes over her and speaks through the medium, who is unaware of what might be happening. When the medium wakes up out of trance, he may not have any memory of the proceedings. No, thank you!

I also was not interested in "physical mediumship" which is when spirits control matter and the phenomena can objectively be sensed by others (objects moving about as if by invisible hands, sights and sounds that everyone in the room can see, hear, or feel). Besides, at that time I was still skeptical about spirit communication through mediums, especially when fraudulent mediums resorted to magic tricks to produce "physical mediumship."

One of the beliefs of Spiritualists that separates them from the general public opinion is that mediumship is NOT a gift from God. Rather, it is a human faculty which can be strengthened through study and practice. Everyone is a medium already. Ta-dah! Some people are born with the talent already sharpened, while others may train for years and achieve mediocre results. Still, others may suppress it, deny it, or ignore it their whole lives. Today, when someone compliments me with, "What a wonderful God-given gift you've demonstrated," I cringe inside. I will politely thank the person for the compliment and patiently explain to them that it's a faculty and not a gift, and that they, too, could do the same thing.

For the sake of clarification, when I refer to a medium in this book, although "everyone is a medium," I am specifically referring to those people who have embraced the term and are consciously using their abilities in either a professional and/or religious manner to find information connected to the dead and to assist the living. This would refer to both student mediums and "working mediums."

One evening, I was enrolled in a workshop at an occult/metaphysical bookstore called The Green Man in North Hollywood, California, which has recently re-opened in the city of Burbank. The workshop was about meeting one's spirit guides. During the meditation, I saw the shoulders and head of a man appear, dressed in white. He was smiling. I received the name "Caelan."

And that was all I received. Whenever I tried checking in on him, I just saw his head and shoulders and a smile without words.

Meanwhile, I was very curious about séances involving mental mediumship. If physical mediumship is about ghosts appearing in front of people at a séance, oozing ectoplasm, or objects moving or levitating, mental mediumship is when the medium verbally produces evidence and communication from the spirits to the living. Television mediums practice mental mediumship.

I figured it was all just Extra Sensory Perception (ESP). Perhaps the medium who brought forth successful and evidential info was simply reading the auric memory of the sitter and mistaking it as the dead loved one coming through.

I started experimenting with conducting séances. I had found an old Spiritualist Manual from the late 1800's from a used book store and followed the directions. It seemed I had mediocre success with the ten-or-more participants that I sometimes experimented with, if I could get that many people to agree to a place and time. But again, I figured this was all just psychic information that I was picking up from their memories.

In 2017, I had an incredible urge to research mediumship further, and I discovered a small Spiritualist church in Monrovia, California. I decided to go.

At first, I thought it was a little corny and campy. I grew up a preacher's kid, since my father graduated from Fuller Theological Seminary, so I was used to visiting many churches. This church mimicked those small "starter churches" with no fellowship hall, no pews, no double doors, and no steeple. It had a platform and a podium. Chairs were arranged in rows with an aisle in the center of the room. The church's administrative desk, computer, phone, and filing cabinets were in the very back. It had a kitchen and two restrooms. It looked like a converted house that might have once been an insurance or dental office.

Being an anthropology graduate, I was more used to the unusual when it came to non-Judeo-Christian practices, like people dancing around bonfires and howling at the moon, or sacrificing chickens to the beat of African drums which I witnessed while visiting northern Brazil. Instead, we sang hymns that were reconstituted 19th century hymns from Christian churches. The invisible accompanying piano was from a CD player. How bland.

The service was conducted in similar fashion to most Christian-based Sunday services. There was a prayer for healing session, then a devotional session with chosen hymns, a sermon, church announcements, the offering plate, and then the "Messages From Spirits." A medium stood up on the platform and asked permission from members of the congregation if they would like a message from Spirit. You always had to ask permission, first.

After the closing prayer and hymn, I suddenly remembered my spirit guide Caelan, who never said anything or revealed to me the rest of his body. I had almost forgotten about him. But there in the church parking lot, I saw him in my inner eye. I now saw him from head to toes, and he finally spoke with the words, "Hello Russell. I'm glad you came to visit this little church. The reason I am here is to help and assist you in becoming a medium."

Um...OK, Caelan.

Chapter Two

Who Might Be Interested in This Book?

Two teachers and church elders, the late Reverend Martin Pena, and the retired Reverend Ernest Leard, told me that all student mediums should keep a journal or log, especially of one's successes and learning moments. Successes are important because there will be some days when you don't feel your best and you might need an occasional reminder that, yes, you can still do this, and you've done it successfully before.

When I've walked into the homes of some police officers, I've seen award certificates and trophies, framed commendations, and shadow boxes on shelves and walls. In a way, these awards, like the journal, are reminders of one's positive abilities and accomplishments. If you think this might seem like unnecessary boasting, imagine walking into a room in your own home on which hangs on the walls framed complaints, bad report cards, break-up letters, hate mail, and trophies stating "Number 1 Loser" or other reminders of one's failures. Feel any better? Not very nurturing, is it?

What started as a journal, turned into an email blog, which I shared with sworn and civilian employees who had a secret, or not-so-secret, interest in psychic phenomena and mediumship. I gave it the title, "True Tales From the Platform." What started as a journal for myself, turned into a book to share with others.

So, other than the general public interested in mediums and spirits, whom else might find this interesting?

Reasonable Skeptics

This book is for the reasonable skeptic. Maybe you are still questioning if the personality still exists after death, or maybe you are questioning the whole concept of the paranormal. I started out doing mediumship readings for skeptics. I'll explain.

Being a practical and somewhat skeptical Taurus, after joining the police department in May of 2000, I kept my "woo-woo" tolerance factor to a low number, meaning that I didn't view all that "supernatural stuff" as anything that I wanted to delve into, unless I thought it had a very practical application and that it could help myself and others in a practical and meaningful way.

Sure, UFO's, ghosts, Bigfoot, and such were fun and fascinating to study, but I preferred topics that could perhaps bring healing to others, or offer help to others.

My goal after stumbling upon the little church in 2017 was to become a Platform Medium at the Spiritualist Church of Revelation (SCoR), which is part of the National Spiritualist Association of Churches (NSAC). This requires the student to stand on the church platform in front of the congregation and deliver messages from the spirit world to specific individuals, usually during a Sunday morning church service. I wanted to know if someone's personality actually survived death and if communication were actually possible, versus reading the memories of loved ones out of someone's aura or memory.

If you think it might be nerve-wracking to stay in the correct frame of mind when doing a reading one-on-one in a private space, imagine doing this while everyone is looking at you while you stand on a stage or platform. Not only must you conquer stage fright, you must remain centered within your power, trust the spirit world, and speak well enough so that the entire room/sanctuary/meeting hall can hear you, AND hope that whatever you say turns out to be accurate evidence confirmed by the sitter. Reading fortune cookies would be so much easier!

In order to build confidence, I needed willing guinea pigs to practice on. But, I didn't want to do readings for any of my metaphysical friends. Reading for friends and family seems like tainted evidence to me. You already know enough about them, and it's hard to tell if what you are receiving is simply one's own subconscious biased material. The same goes for friends who also study and practice occult and paranormal things — they might be too forgiving due to their high "woo-woo" levels.

No. I wanted to read for people I did not know.

People who might be naturally skeptical and "woo-woo" avoidant.

People who were on the fence on the subject of life continuing after death.

People who could keep a straight, emotionless face, without giving away any body language, which can subconsciously affect the medium's mind.

People who would know if you were intentionally trying to fool them.

People who might appear standoffish and somewhat intimidating at first meeting.

The answer was easy: my fellow cop co-workers. I figured if I could do accurate readings in reuniting them with known departed family and friends with confidence, then I would be ready for the public.

Another reason I thought about giving free readings to officers and coworkers was because of the LAPD's motto, "To Protect and To Serve." Perhaps this was one of the ways I could return service to them beyond the clerical tasks which I got paid for. Also, many of them take a dim view of "fortune tellers" and are rather suspicious (or even scared) of anything smacking of "woo-woo" and possible fraud. Perhaps I could provide them new possibilities and a broader perspective that not everyone in this "business" are frauds or delusional. Because what do Spiritualist mediums and police have in common? We look for evidence.

Since I eventually gained positive responses and evidential feedback from the police, after already establishing my strong work ethic and garnering awards, I was finally brave enough to take on the platform at SCoR-NSAC in Monrovia and start working for credentials.

Student Mediums

I don't claim to be some master teacher of mediumship. In fact, compared to those mediums who grew up demonstrating their talents at an early age, I'd say I am a "toddler medium" since I began to pursue Spiritualism and mediumship at the tender age of 49.

But, during the time that I was reading for my coworkers, I was technically already a student medium. I was enrolled in the course to become a Certified Medium through the Morris Pratt Institute (MPI), which is the educational arm of the NSAC. If the Jesuits are the educational arm of the Roman Catholic Church, and Brigham Young University is the educational arm of the Mormons, the MPI provides credentials for people to become certified in the NSAC as ministers, mediums, spiritual healers, teachers, etc. Mediumship certification requires a lot of writing assignments and proof-of-mediumship affidavits, along with examinations.

In my mind, I had a 3-step plan.

Step 1: By gaining confidence in reading for the police in a one-on-one private setting, I would have confidence to do public platform readings at the church.

Step 2: Whenever I was accurate enough at church, a satisfied sitter could fill out an affidavit for me. We encourage members and visitors who have had a positive and accurate reading to fill out an affidavit for those student mediums working on their certification. I would need a certain number of affidavits turned in to the NSAC headquarters in Lily Dale, New York, which is required as part of earning my certification.

Step 3: Turn in the required amount of signed affidavits, plus turning in all the essay paperwork, plus passing the preliminary open-book written exam, plus passing the closed-book written exam in front of 3 NSAC proctors, equals finally gaining my Certified Medium credentials. Whew! No wonder so many mediums became alcoholics!

As far as teaching mediumship, I found myself teaching and facilitating mediumship development circles following the Sunday morning church services, both while I was a student, and after earning my credentials in October of 2021. I was also leading development circles online during the Coronavirus Pandemic, through a Canadian Spiritualist church located in Burnaby, British Columbia. Since I earned my credentials in 2021, and my home church stayed closed in 2020 (no one was computer-savvy to go online), I was a student teaching other students out of necessity.

Nothing irks older, more experienced, "elder" mediums more than when novice mediums suddenly feel they can hang up their business sign right away after demonstrating a few successes and sporting a "know-it-all" attitude. I certainly don't claim to be an "elder medium" and this book is coming from the viewpoint of a student medium sharing his personal experiences to interested readers.

So, most of the material in this book is written by a student, which can then be shared with other students.

But even after receiving my credentials, in my opinion, we are always going to be students for the rest of our lives.

For Spiritual Seekers Looking For a Simpler Path

Perhaps you are a person who already believes in psychic abilities and has strong hunches, and are further interested in exploring the continuance of the personality after the transition called death. Maybe you are a psychic who is trying to separate the abilities of ESP and accurate spirit communication. Or, perhaps you are a reader who is curious about the possibility of life after death, but from the vantage point of a skeptic.

This book is for you. The journal entries are based on the years from 2017 (when I started) to before my job retirement in 2023 and are already a part of my email blog, "True Tales From the Platform." Most of the entries were during the earlier years, and fewer in the later years after gaining my credentials. So much has happened within those years to a relative novice who is also skeptical. Meaning, if I could do these things, so can you.

I can hear other spiritual-skeptics disapproving of some guy claiming that he can do all this stuff in just a matter of a few years. Where is the intense training lasting decades? Where are the years of harsh discipline and pain? What do you mean he didn't have to meditate on a mountaintop in snow, surviving on a pot of jasmine tea??

Well...what I have found to be different with learning mediumship in the Spiritualist tradition is that less is more. It's not so much about continually adding to one's tool kit, like a shaman acquiring animal and plant totems, a drum, bones and feathers, or purchasing crystals and copper pyramids and becoming vegan, but stripping away one's own inner blockages and preconceptions to be a more open channel.

I was learning how to "un-learn" things to become a better medium.

Sure, there are mediums who love collecting crystal balls, Tarot cards, wands, minerals, herbs, and magical candles, but in actual, evidential mediumship, none of these are necessary. The Fox Sisters in 1848, Hydesville, New York, weren't using any of these fancy items when they first established communication with a deceased peddler who happened to have been murdered and buried in their cellar before they moved in...they weren't chanting to archangels under a suspended pyramid or studying the chakra system, or casting magic circles on their cabin floor with Latin and Hebrew phrases written in chalk. They were underaged girls living in a farm cabin with a recovering-alcoholic father and their open-minded mother.

Just to be clear, the NSAC does not "corner the mediumship market." Mediums have existed in many cultures through the centuries. Some channel ancient cultural deities and avatars, while others channel extraterrestrial intelligences. Some are in touch with the forces of nature, like The Faerie realms and the Elementals, the angelic realms, or they speak for western Neo-Pagan deities.

They have been called by the following different names and labels: shaman, witch, wise person, magus, healer, medicine person, etc. Many non-Spiritualist mediums use a lot of "material culture" in their mediumship, like special robes and ethnic costumes, swords, fake paper money (called Hell Bank Notes in Asian cultures), different forms of fire/flames, incense, clear glasses of water on a table with a white table cloth, drumming and sound, colognes like Florida Water, divination cards, bundles of herbs, sacred geometry and drawings on the floor, etc.

However, a Spiritualist Medium, particularly in the NSAC, focuses their mediumship on Dead People, especially those that are known and familiar to the living. If a medium is attempting to prove the existence of life after death, it might be more evidential — and healing — to the grieving loved one to hear from the medium some very specific and personal details about their deceased relative that no one else would have known, than to receive a visitation from the Archangel Michael, the Atlanteans, and a Greek dryad (personally, I like Archangel Michael, and many police officers do, too).

I love the minimalism of mental mediumship. I like not having to rely on spiritual props and objects to put the "spirit" back into being spiritual. It makes house cleaning and shelf dusting so much easier. I also prefer the simplicity of providing the sitter with proof of their loved on in spirit through specific details and memories, versus a pronouncement from an entity from another dimension. If this appeals to you, you might still end up spending money...but this would be spent on workshops, books and audio lessons, or maybe a membership fee in a Spiritualist church.

If you went the route of a physical medium, you might spend money on an aluminum trumpet (a thin metallic cone used in multiple ways to indicate movement and spirit voices during a séance), chalk and slates, a séance-worthy table for table-tipping, and recorders for electronic voice phenomenon. But as you can see, these items in themselves aren't culturally iconic. They are less symbolic and more practical. If Wicca and shamanism's values on material culture can be compared to Roman Catholicism's, Spiritualism's *lack* of material culture can be compared to the Quakers or the Methodists.

I did spend money on the MPI course, and I learned that a platform medium at a church needed to wear specific clothing (imagine business casual with a tie). But never was I instructed that I needed to invest in specific jewelry, stones, oils, wands, cards, etc.

I'm not criticizing people for having these items, I have them, too. Maybe not as much as before, since I've been going for the minimalist look at home, but I still enjoy a smaller collection of metaphysical "tchotchkes" for "folk-magic nostalgia." When I became a Spiritualist, I gave a lot of my "tools" away. I just don't use them when practicing mediumship. While gemstones and crystals are not needed to become an effective medium, I still enjoy how pretty they are in my living room.

CHAPTER THREE

How This Book is Organized and How the Readings Were Conducted

Before it became a book, it was an email journal. Yet, certain entries contain bits of wisdom and learning along with things that student mediums might also experience as rather new and surprising for their first time. At the beginning of each entry will be a brief mention of what can be learned from that particular session.

Some of the earlier journal entries from 2017 were unfortunately not dated (my bad!). If I was able to retain the journal dates, they'd be included. The blog entries are reproduced as originally written at the time. If they were edited, it was for clarity.

You will probably notice as you progress through the book that not all journal entries are based on readings for the police. This is due to my confidence building enough so that I was finally willing to "serve the platform" at the church, as was my goal. Still, the journal entries that dealt with readings outside of the Department were still shared with Department employees who were still interested in this topic and supported my pursuit of earning my mediumship credentials.

Gray block side notes include practical information and further background information that was not included in the email blogs.

The sitters included in this book started primarily with co-workers, then branched out to people outside of work.

How did I manage doing some of the readings while at work? Sometimes, we would conduct the reading during a 15-minute required break, inside an interrogation room with the door closed and locked, and a sign stating "Room In Use." The other way was through my role as a Peer Support Counselor.

Behavioral Sciences Services (BSS) is the Department's psychology division. Many cops are wary of having to visit a psychologist, but sometimes they are ordered to go, especially when a shooting or traumatic event is involved.

But what about the non-emergencies of the daily grind? BSS came up with an idea to train volunteer employees to become Peer Support Counselors. You didn't have to be a doctor or trained in psychology, but there was a week-long training on how to listen to people without judgement. Both sworn and civilian volunteers took the course and found it useful. Now, an employee could approach any Peer Support Counselor on an informal basis in confidentiality, at any time, in any location, in person or over the phone, without the pressure of visiting BSS.

The program became so successful that at the annual March training luncheons, we had sworn visitors from other police agencies around the country attend because they wanted to bring our program back to their agencies.

I don't remember who suggested that I enroll in the program, but someone recommended me as a candidate. Since my Myers-Briggs Personality is "INFP", it seemed like a natural pairing. The "INFP" personality trait is one of 16 in the Myers-Briggs Type Indicator and is one of the rarer personalities. We are sometimes labeled "The Mediator" and "The Healer."

From one's own personal experiences, a Peer Support Counselor could list their specialties on the available roster. Some employees had experiences with death of a child or parent, some had experiences enduring a complaint investigation on the job. Some had experiences with LGBTQ-related problems, alcoholism, divorce, and other topics. I guess I became the "spook counselor" even though I did not list my specialty as such.

No worries — Infinite Intelligence (God/Creator) brings together people that are meant to meet each other. Somehow, I found myself bringing closure to sworn employees surrounding the death of their loved ones, and giving them a new way to view our existence as humans in life and in death. Also, while I was working at COMPSTAT, I had a police sergeant across the hallway in Communications Division who suffered from being a wide-open, un-trained medium, who did not know how to shut down his ability, let alone understand this amazing faculty. I was able to assist him in learning to shut down, set boundaries with eager spirits, and control his mediumship abilities.

What about that female spirit with the pale skin and light freckles who dropped in because she wanted me to reach out to that Detective

Supervisor (the spirit's descendant) mentioned in the prologue? Her situation will have her own entry.

But, let's start at the beginning..

CHAPTER FOUR

My First "Guinea Pig"

One of the interesting learning points was separating two spirits standing very close together, and trying not to leave any specific details out. Later, I learned that if you believe that two spirits have appeared together, that you can just ask them to separate, then have one of them step forward first.

When: unknown, summer of 2017

Dear Readers,

I sat down with Police Officer II "Edward" in the break room on the 3rd floor of the Police Headquarters Facility (PHF). I explained to Edward that I could not guarantee who would come through to him, but that I would do my best.

I said a prayer, visualized the circulation of energy in my body, and saw a woman pointing to her chest indicating that her death was affected by her chest. The word "cancer" appeared in my head, and she indicated that she passed away in her mid-40's. She stood behind Edward's right shoulder (my left), so I said that this woman was from his mother's side of the family.

[Later in this book, I discuss the spirit's relationship to the sitter via how the spirit "stands" in relation to the sitter, like behind right/left shoulders, etc.]

She handed him a crucifix.

She looked like she was bending over to speak to children, trying to comfort them and saying things like, "Don't worry, they'll be back soon. They'll return and come for you."

I also saw Hispanic folk art pottery/figurines in the house on display. Edward confirmed that these items were in the kitchen.

I saw Mom and Dad telling each other jokes and cracking each other up. Then, Mom was cursing out or scolding a car. To me, the vehicle appeared to be blue, but I left this information out.

Then, onto Edward's left shoulder, an old man appeared with a big mustache, dressed in a nice white suit, black and white hair, bad leg, bad walk. Gray eyes with cataracts. Edward explained that it could have been his grandfather who had all-white hair, whereas his dead uncle had the black and white hair. His grandfather had the bad leg and walk, so a special shoe was made with a few inches added on to the heel to give him more height on the bad leg.

I asked Edward if there was someone he really wanted to hear from. He replied his mother. So, I asked if she was present and I received a woman who was coughing...A LOT. It was that same woman described earlier, in her mid-40's. Edward confirmed that his mother died coughing heavily and that she passed at the age of 45. Before the coffin was closed, a crucifix was removed from her coffin and given to Edward. His mother had a sense of humor. The image of her comforting children was probably something she was doing from heaven, because Edward's children had abandonment issues, and his wife was the one having to comfort them when Dad was on the job.

Hours later, when Officer Edward was packing up to go home, I asked him, "Hey...maybe you can confirm from your older sister if your mother ever chastised a BLUE car."

Edward replied, "Hey...Mom's car was blue! But I never mentioned the color."

When we were both walking out of the office, Edward asked me if the same spirits ever show up in future sessions? I think he was possibly interested in seeing me again to unite him with his mother. His mother died when he was 14 years old. He also wondered out loud if his work-partner would also be interested in doing a sitting. I took it that Spirit and I did a decent job for a beginner.

You might notice me mentioning "P II, P III, Detective Supervisor, etc." These are ranks and pay grades within ranks of the sworn in LAPD. I don't know how other police agencies organize their ranks, other than a police officer is below a sergeant, and a sergeant is below a lieutenant, etc.
All sworn begin as a Police Officer I, sometimes referred to as P I or PO I. These are also the probationers, some still in the Academy,

others riding around with training officers in the field. A PO I must graduate and pass probation in order to stay on the job as sworn.

Police Officer II – After graduating and passing their probation, a police officer automatically becomes a PO II and gets a better paycheck. They can remain this rank for the rest of their career.

Police Officer III – A pay grade. PO III's carry more responsibilities. They can end up training probationers, or get involved in community affairs. In the Old Days, you had to be a "P III + 1" in order to join the ranks of the Mounted Unit of Metropolitan Division (the cops who ride horses and get to wear cowboy hats), and other units within "Metro." I've explained "Metro Division" to my civilian friends as our "Calendar Cops" — meaning if we had to print an unofficial calendar showing off our most fit male and female officers in flattering gym wear or bathing suits, we would pull them from Metro, due to the stringent PFQ (Physical Fitness Qualification) in order to make the grade. You won't see donuts on these cops. If, in an alternate parallel universe, I was a police officer, I'd never make it into Metro because I love food too much!

Sergeant I and II – When I was working in Office of Operations, our Sergeant I's would usually supervise one of our admin units. When I worked PM Watch at Foothill Division, we sometimes had a Sergeant II working the Watch Commander's office.

Detectives I, II, III – Some sworn would end up in detectives. The 21 Area Divisions (Area Divisions is how we say "police stations" or "precincts") each have their own detective section, and Police Headquarters Facility has Detective Bureau with all its many specialty divisions, like Juvenile Division, Gangs and Narcotics, Robbery-Homicide, Financial Crimes, etc. When I retired, COMPSTAT Division was answering to Detective Bureau.

Lieutenant I, II – There is an unofficial saying in LAPD that I've heard in the hallways that if you want to become a Captain, there are two ways to almost guarantee this. First, become the Officer-in-Charge (OIC) of an Area Division's detective section. The second way is to be the Lieutenant II (OIC) of the Evaluation and Administration Section of Office of Operations (OO). I can personally vouch for the second method. Having worked 9.5 years in OO, I have seen every Lieutenant II eventually become a Captain and higher, except for one. That one Lieutenant was the one who brought me into OO, and it was his personal decision to eventually retire as the OIC over Devonshire Area Division's detective side. I had the pleasure of attending his retirement party and meeting his family.

Captain I, II, III – Outside of the 21 Area Divisions, there are many divisions that operate in the LAPD that don't function as "neighborhood police stations." These divisions are usually under a Captain I or II. The top sworn of an Area Division is usually a Captain III. Captains and above are salaried, whereas lieutenants and below have an hourly wage. I am especially familiar with this because I was a Timekeeper for many years, which I enjoyed.

Commander – A Commander can be responsible for a Bureau which contains a number of Area Divisions.

Deputy Chief, Assistant Chief – They can be responsible for an Office, which is higher than a Bureau. They also answer to the Chief.

Chief of Police – This is the top sworn position. The Chief answers to the Mayor and to the Board of Police Commissioners. While working in the Office of the Chief of Police, I served under one chief retiring, and under one incoming who promoted from Assistant Chief.

Chapter Five

Testing the Spirits

Dear Reader,

It's always a good idea to "test the spirits" especially those that are not your lifetime guides and guardian angels. Even the Bible mentions doing this. This is why in Spiritualism, we ask for evidence and facts we can verify. Or, at least a sign. We don't want to attract a trickster, or be deluded by our "imagination."

Before going to bed, I had finished reading a chapter from a book about contacting one's spirit guides. Although I certainly have guides, I was more curious about the meditation technique (there are actually many). So, during meditation, I followed the instructions and was expecting one of my known guides to appear. But no...I met an unusual guide. The instructions said to imagine a door that lifted slowly, instead of opening from the side. As the door lifts, see your guide's feet. This one was wearing sandals or flip-flops. As the door slowly lifts more, you look at what s/he is wearing, and finally, the entire body.

The guide that stood before me reminded me of Hollywood celebrity, Chuck McCarthy, the People Walker. Or, any young Grateful Dead/hippie fan.

The guide went by the name "Farnsworth." Um...OK.

I asked him what his role was because he didn't seem to be a Protector, Healer, Fact Finder, etc. In a very laid-back voice, he said that he was here to assist me with learning how to chill and have more fun in life. I retorted in a supercilious tone that I was already having fun in my life and didn't need to "learn how to chill," dammit!

Oops, caught red-handed. One point for Farnsworth.

I explained that he needed to prove to me that he was what he claimed. In my mind's eye, I saw him get up (he was sitting to my left at one point), and proceeded to juggle common round fruits, like apples and oranges.

"Look, I can juggle!" he exclaimed. That's pretty good, I thought. I can't juggle anything. Farnsworth said that the next day, he would send me a sign related somehow to juggling. Tomorrow?? Hmm...fat chance. In downtown L.A., we don't really have street performers except the odd musician, but even that is rare. And, I don't go out of my way to look at juggling acts on YouTube. Even when I attend the Renaissance Fair in Irwindale, CA, I don't usually sit down to watch the juggling stage shows.

I "shook hands" with him and got ready for bed.

The next morning, I forgot all about the night before.

Sometime before 7:00 a.m., one of our sergeants from Chief of Staff came into my office to say "hi." He is originally from The Ukraine. He went over to my coworker's desk and was showing her a video. I couldn't see the video, but I could hear it. A Ukrainian man was being interviewed. When asked what he was about to do before the audience, he said, "I am a JUGGLER." You could then hear the admiration from the audience as he proceeded with his act.

Suddenly, the night before came flooding back – nay, smacking me upside the head. And this was almost first thing in the morning, not later in the day.

After experiencing this world for well over 35+ years when I embarked on this path as a teenager, I have learned that "coincidences" can have meaning. As for Farnsworth, I have a feeling he has a more important role to play besides just chilling and having fun.

You, Too, Can Test the Spirits

Mediums are often accused of being delusional, which is totally understandable. As a skeptic who has worked for a skeptical governmental organization, I have constantly had to do "reality checks" on myself while getting involved with churches and organizations deemed "woo-woo" to outsiders. That's why, when researching on becoming a medium, I wanted to go into Spiritualist mediumship because they primarily deal with Dead People and evidential mediumship.

It's not enough for a medium to simply declare, "I have your dead grandmother here and she wants to send you her love." That's nice and all, but to be credible, the medium needs to back up this statement

with evidence that only the sitter would understand about Dead
Grandma. The same holds true for spirits claiming to be your spirit
guides.

Test the spirits. Give them a reasonable task to accomplish within
a reasonable amount of time, occurring in the material "mundane"
world. In the case of Farnsworth, my Joy Guide, he even volunteered
to fulfill his task the very next day...I did not ask for that specific a
time period, so I was impressed when he specifically said "tomorrow"
and then proved it before the rest of the West Coast was waking up.
How do you ask? In the same way you would text or speak to a friend.
Ask out loud, or write it down.

CHAPTER SIX

The Detective Supervisor and the Surprise Visit

Remember the female spirit with the pale skin, light freckles, looking just like the Detective Supervisor working on the 9th Floor in Police Headquarters?

This two-parter story is actually an example of something the Morris Pratt Institute course defines as "advance clairvoyance." The word "advance" does not refer to a superior level of expertise. Instead, it means receiving a message *in advance* of actually meeting the sitter.

Advance Clairvoyance means that a spirit is not communicating through you as a medium to the living loved one. Instead, the medium turns into an answering service or a digital recorder to be used by the spirit. The spirit leaves the message, then "departs." It's up to the medium who is "stuck" with the message to contact the living and relay that message at a later time. It's "close-but-no-cigar" mediumship. Some teachers don't care for advance clairvoyance because it isn't true mediumship — true mediumship is when all three parties are actually together at the exact same time communicating.

But, advance clairvoyance does happen, and other Spiritualists are totally for it. Mediumship can sometimes be difficult and an imperfect science, so to receive ANY accurate message even at a later date or time is better than receiving nothing at all in the present time,

This story also teaches not editing oneself, because the first information you receive is usually correct.

Part 1

Dear Readers,

Sometimes I enjoy visiting the round garden next to the police Memorial Wall, built above Señor Fish Restaurant. It's the closest thing PHF has to a garden, and it reminds me of a hymn we sing in the Spiritualist Church that starts, "I come to the garden alone, when the dew is still on the roses..."

Lately, I've been receiving spirit visitors there. I told Jim about this. He is wondering if it's because I'm near the Memorial Wall? Of course, spirits can show up anywhere. You don't have to be hanging out in a graveyard, mausoleum, or a memorial wall for them to show up.

Today was a rather unusual lunch break. As I was enjoying the storm clouds, I saw a female spirit to the left of my peripheral vision. She looked vaguely familiar. I asked my Gatekeeper Guide if this spirit was meant to reach out to me, and he nodded as if to say, "It's OK, take the call."

I asked her whom she was related to and I immediately got the name of a detective supervisor who works on the 9th floor of PHF. This made sense because this spirit looked just like the detective – the hair had more red than blonde, perhaps a gentle shade darker. The complexion was the same, down to small freckles, the hair worn above the shoulders, the eyes were the same. No wonder the spirit looked familiar! The detective supervisor that this spirit resembled was once a police officer whom I worked with back at Foothill Division in the early 2000's. And now, almost 20 years later, she promoted to the 9th floor.

I asked for a relationship (I'm still working on this). In my mind's eye, the spirit stood behind the detective's right shoulder, or my left side. This would indicate that the spirit was either the detective's mother, or a close maternal aunt. I shuddered at the possibility that it was her mother and instead went with "maternal aunt". NOTE: Don't edit what you receive…usually the first response is the correct response, as you will soon see…

What message did this woman have for the detective? I immediately saw a car engine in front of me. Not the car, just the engine. To me, it meant bringing in your car for servicing or maintenance. It could mean an engine light coming on in the dashboard. And, that's all I felt – nothing deeply spiritual.

But, what freaked me out about this visitation is that while I know the recipient from years ago, this detective has no clue that I've been pursuing this path. I don't want to look stupid. But, when you follow this path, it's a sacred responsibility you have, regardless of what your Ego fears about being ridiculed, being called a fake or fraud, etc. It's one thing to deliver a message to someone who has experienced it first-hand with me, and to someone who has some belief in what I do. But, it's another to deliver it to a stranger who might not understand, or have very cynical, negative beliefs about anything "woo-woo."

As I walked back to my office, I devised a simple plan. Just email the detective and say that I had an odd question to ask her. Please call me on my cell phone or my office line.

She called.

I hesitated, but explained to her what I was doing with the church, my working towards certification, and the visitation this afternoon. I told her that I felt embarrassed that I was sticking my neck out on a chopping block, but... did she lose a maternal aunt?

No, but her mother passed away 6 months ago (I should have went by my first impression — lesson learned). Yes, her mother looked the way I described, and yes, she dressed in light colors/pastels, like it was Easter. Yes, her hair had more red, she had a few freckles and her complexion matched her daughter's and, yes, her hair was worn above the shoulder.

The detective couldn't think about whether her vehicle/s needed servicing, but her father just took his car in for repairs. She was actually pleased that I called her, and she missed her mother a lot. No, she didn't think I was "crazy" for doing what I was doing. And while I certainly don't think that I am, she thought I was an angel! She would keep a look-out on her car/s. Other than that, her mom was smiling and looking like she just had a spring stroll through a garden – very refreshed.

After I ended the call, I gave thanks to my guide and to the spirit-mother of the detective.

Mediumship is a continual journey of learning to listen and to trust – and the main reason for it is to show how love continues as a positive force in the universe.

Part 2

Dear Readers,

My advisors recommended that I document my mediumship sessions. It's interesting when receiving confirmation right there and then. What's more interesting is when confirmations either arrive more detailed and pertinent, at a later time, or when the confirmation comes through a third party.

If you recall, I received information for a detective supervisor working in PHF from her recently-deceased mother. I shared the information I received over the phone with her.

The last bit of information I received was a floating car engine in front of me. Coincidentally, her father had just taken his car in for maintenance. End of session.

What I forgot to document was what happened the next day.

The detective supervisor emailed me back, asking me if the engine that I saw was a car engine or a motorcycle engine. Not being a mechanic, I told her that I assumed it was a car engine, but that it looked much smaller than any car engine I have ever seen. Also, it looked "old" or "vintage" – it didn't look anything like my Prius engine or anything computerized. Still, to have a spirit disappear in front of you and be replaced by a floating gas engine in space is a weird message to give to anyone. It made no sense to me.

Her response to me was:

"Thanks so much for all the information. I asked about the engine because my mom was given a 1972 Kawasaki from my dad. We grew up riding it and have only amazing memories of it. For the past couple of weeks, my husband completely took it apart & has been restoring it. A couple of days ago, he took pictures of the engine, exhaust, etc. and sent it to my brother-in-law with a caption "L— — — [I removed her name] (my mom) is back alive and [with] you." It gave me the chills.

"As for the hands over the chest. She was a heavy smoker but refused to see a doctor the last couple of years." [In an earlier email specifically to the detective supervisor, I mentioned that the spirit put her hands over her chest, indicating a complication with the lungs or breasts.]

This was a good lesson that the medium is not always the message. We might receive information that doesn't make sense, or information that we feel might make us look stupid because it doesn't seem logical to us. But, the telephone doesn't question or judge the information that the caller is giving to the receiver.

As for advance clairvoyance? It can come at any time if you haven't set proper boundaries. I was once driving to church when a spirit dropped in and wanted me to pass along a message.

Another time, I was busy preparing food for my pressure cooker in my California condo about 45 minutes before I was to lead an online Spiritualist evening service based in British Columbia, Canada. While chopping the vegetables, the spirit of a man dropped in saying that his sitter would be online that evening and to make sure I gave his message to her. When I asked who the sitter was, I received no answer from him.

Oh, great, just great. I do not enjoy "indirect approach" mediumship because the NSAC only taught us "direct approach." Indirect approach means that you throw out the spirit's description into the audience and hope that someone will "claim the information." The NSAC discourages this approach and wants their mediums to do "direct approach" — meaning, you address a specific sitter and relay the information. Although the online church service was not NSAC, I still did as I was taught.

Pressure cooker set to cook, when I finally logged into the online conference platform and it came time for messages, I scrolled and swiped through the different faces, wondering who the heck was this mysterious sitter that the spook said would be there? My eyes rested on a visitor whom I've never met before. She had logged in from Toronto and it was her first visit to the Canadian church. A total stranger. This was the recipient. Although the male spirit never told me who it was, I just had that inner feeling that it was her. When I relayed the gentleman's information, down to his cigarette-smelling light-blue buttoned shirts, and one-upmanship strong personality, she knew exactly who it was and was grateful for the connection.

Just Who's Side Are You On?

Mediums need a way to figure out how a spirit is related to the sitter. Some techniques involve clairaudience in which the spirit simply tells the medium, "Hey...I was the sitter's second husband." But not all mediums are clairaudient in that way.
Some mediums use a technique in which their own friends or relatives appear in their mind to indicate a parallel relationship.

So, if a female spirit appears and then my female cousin (who is very much alive) comes to my mind, then I would say that the spirit coming to you

happens to be your dead cousin. However, this doesn't always work, especially if the visiting spirit was a sibling, and the medium is an only child. I come from a small family, so I have no filing-cabinet references for brothers and sisters.

So, the technique which I prefer is called "spirit placement." Someone told me that many British mediums use this technique. Nothing works 100% perfectly, but this is my go-to technique. If I am looking directly at the sitter or client across from me, I discern the spirit's relationship to the sitter according to the following positions the spirit takes while "standing" near the sitter:

- Behind sitter's right shoulder (my left), mother's side of the family. Further back and up, maternal grandparents, great-grandparents, etc.

- Behind sitter's left shoulder (my right), father's side of the family. Further back and up, paternal grandparents,, great-grandparents, etc.

- In front of the sitter, deceased children, which can sometimes include miscarriages. Sometimes the child is nestled under the sitter's chin or resting on their shoulder in the front.

- Directly behind the sitter and elevated, or floating above the sitter's head - spirit guides.

- Deceased pets are all over the place. Dogs and cats running up and down the church aisles, birds flying near the ceiling, perched on book shelves, snakes slithering between the chairs, etc.

CHAPTER SEVEN

The Police Officer's Wife

If you are doing a reading for someone and you feel that their facial expressions and body language might be too distracting, I suggest doing your reading "blind." This can be done over the phone, or by simply keeping your eyes closed when in person. The sitter's proximity to the medium is not necessary for an effective reading, nor is watching the sitter's bodily and facial expressions. Also, a spirit (unlike a "ghost") is not limited to a specific place, like a house, cemetery, or battle field. So, the reading can be conducted without the medium and the sitter being in the same room.

Since I was still rather new to all this, in this session, I kept my eyes closed during the reading.

Before proceeding, I'll introduce the key people. Officer "Terry" is a Japanese-American friend of mine. Her Hispanic working partner is Officer "Mann". Officer Mann is married and I will call his wife Mrs. Mann. Together, the Mann's have three sons.

Two Weeks Earlier...

Terry – [paraphrased text message to Russell] "Hey Russell, the wife of my partner Officer Mann is having her birthday, and she's interested in seeing a medium to contact any family members on the Other Side. I told Mann that you were doing this and he'd like to set up an appointment between you and his wife. However, it's a birthday secret and I'll pay you."

I knew Officer Mann because occasionally he went out to eat with us, but I never met his wife. I texted Officer Terry back and we tried to figure out where to meet. Not my place…it's chaotic with all the painting being done in every room and the insides of the closets. I didn't want to do the session at the Mann's house because there would be too many visual clues in the home, like family photos, etc. The less I know, the better the session, I feel. And, since it was between friends/co-workers, I felt I needed to leave out the middle-man (The Green Man Store, who does my bookings, even if I'm not in California). So, I suggested we do it at the home of my friend, Officer Terry.

When: Saturday, August 18, 2018…

On the day of, I brought Jim along with me since we were all going out to lunch together after the session (minus The Mann's). I figured when we got started, Terry and her sister (also a police officer), and her sister's husband could take Jim out for coffee so I would have privacy with Mrs. Mann.

When I entered Terry's home, I shook hands with Officer Mann and his wife. I asked Mrs. Mann if she knew the reason I was here, and she said yes (at some point her husband had to reveal the surprise to her).

"Feel free to light some incense, Russell," said Terry as she, her sister, her brother in law, and Jim left to go get coffee. I found some incense near a Japanese ancestral shrine. After lighting some incense, I sat down with Mrs. Mann at the dining table and explained to her that I was only a Student at my church and that I could not guarantee anything nor anyone specific.

She agreed. I also told her that she was not to say anything to me during the reading. I might occasionally ask for confirmation, and simple "yes" or "no" would suffice. No further details...there would be time later to confirm any notes. I personally wondered if I would be able to do this...we didn't set a specific time limit, and the longest I've ever read was approximately 40 minutes, and that was over the telephone. At the church, it was simply 5 minutes or less per person in the congregation.

I had already said my prayers in the car on the way over, so I began scribbling on a blank notepad. When I felt the first connection, I put down the pen, closed my eyes as usual, and began speaking.

The first person to show up was a woman in vintage clothing, quite colorful. It matched her lipstick. And, oh show she loved to dance. Her skirt would swirl in big circles like Marilyn Monroe. I received the image of cherries, like decorative prints on her clothes, or her jewelry. But the cherry opened up by itself and the juice spilled out, looking rather ominous. Something was wrong with her blood when she passed. It could be diabetes, but no...something else with the blood. And, a man showed up. I described the way he would lounge in a white tank top, but still wearing pleated dress pants. The man gave Mrs. Mann a gift when she was young...I kept seeing the image of "Betty Boop."

A more colorful woman appeared. She changed the color of her hair. She appeared rather avant-garde and more "free" than those around her. I explained that I saw this "auntie" talking to Mrs. Mann as a younger girl, and the other family members would silently disapprove or look out the corners of their eyes just to make sure this "auntie" wasn't corrupting the young Mrs. Mann.

The "auntie" then gave Mrs. Mann some "marital advice" *ahem* to keep her husband happy, which is not suitable to type here. Hey…I'm just the medium. But, I did open my eyes at one point, and Mrs. Mann was smiling. I then saw wine bottles and martini glasses…did your auntie enjoy her drink? Oh yes…she apparently did. When the aunt passed, I saw numerous pills of different colors and shapes, and the wrong combinations of these with drink, which Mrs. Mann confirmed.

My memory is still a little sketchy about last Saturday, except for the last spirit to come through.

The last spirit was sooo small. She tugged at the hem of Mrs. Mann's dress/shirt/jeans, looked up at her pleadingly, then kept pointing at a direction. In my mind's eye, the direction led to a field of yellow flowers, like daisies and sunflowers, with mountains behind. Then, I saw a small, white coffin. I felt this little girl passed from one of those rare childhood diseases that modern medicine missed. I explained to Mrs. Mann that the field of yellow flowers and the mountains reminded me of The Summerland (the old-fashioned Victorian term for "stop-over Heaven" where spirits go to rest before continuing their journey upwards…it's always filled with flowers and fresh water). The tiny girl explained that to go to this field of flowers would bring peace to the heart. Mrs. Mann

44

semi-joked and asked, "Russell, I hope this means I'm not gonna' die soon!"

"No," I explained. "I don't think this little girl's spirit is trying to pull you into Heaven. I think she's trying to explain that to her, this place indicates a place of peace and beauty. For her, and for you. Besides, I don't predict the death of my clients."

"Russell, can you get a name from this girl?"

Normally, I don't get names of people. I'm not that clairaudient. And in the living world, I can barely remember the names of anyone. And, who was the little girl, anyway?? I don't normally see spirit children. But, most of our limitations are self-imposed, so I tuned with my eyes still closed...

"I'm getting a sound like 'Gloria' or 'Aurelia'...either way, the name sounds like it has 'o' and 'r' and '-ia' in the last syllables."

"Yes, that's correct, Russell. The little girl's name is __________," said Mrs. Mann. I don't remember the actual name because it sounded very original and made-up, but it did have those letters at the end of the name. I asked this little girl if she could confirm something about Mrs. Mann? She showed me a transparent pencil case from Mrs. Mann's childhood. It had pink and purple zipper edges, and pink/purple patterns on the see-through plastic part. The little spirit girl wanted Mrs. Mann to take out the colored crayons and markers and color with her. With my eyes still closed, I heard Mrs. Mann laugh as she remembered owning such a pencil case.

I felt it was time to say farewell to the spirits and to give them thanks for showing up. After giving thanks, I opened my eyes and looked at my watch — it had been about 55 minutes. I immediately texted Terry and her sister that we were officially done and to please return with Jim. I don't know why, but I always feel a little self-conscious and weird hanging out with the client after we are finished. I think it might be all that raw emotion from the client. It's one thing for them to be crying during the session, because I'm busy working and my mind is elsewhere. And while I am sensitive (well…it goes without saying…the term "sensitive" also refers to a psychic or medium), I've been working for LAPD for so long that I've gained a callousness around my aura and tend to feel somewhat less comfortable around "messy feelings" than I did before my hire date of May 2000.

"Umm…am I allowed to speak, Russell?" Oops…I did tell her that she was not to speak to me during the sitting. But now, she could.

She confirmed her first two relatives. The woman would dance up a storm and wore colorful prints. The cherry oozing the blood indicated that she indeed passed away from a blood-related disease that was not diabetes.

The man with the tank top gave her a Betty Boop doll which she still owned.

The odd aunt turned out to be her step-aunt who was quite rich and therefore could afford all those gourmet wines. Because she was wealthy, she was able to speak her mind and be more "eccentric" and "open-minded" than her poorer cousins – enough to give practical "marital advice" from the Beyond. She was the one who mixed alcohol with medications.

The final spirit who came through – the little girl tugging at Mrs. Mann's clothes and pointing to the field of flowers and the mountains – was Mrs. Mann's daughter who died very young and was buried in a small, white coffin. Although The Mann's had three boys, and Officer Mann never even mentioned his deceased daughter in any conversation, there wasn't a day that went by that Mrs. Mann didn't remember her daughter. She told me she started crying when I described her (my eyes were closed, so I didn't know she was crying). The place the daughter was pointing to was actually a field behind their home – an empty field with sunflowers and wild daisies, with mountains. Mrs. Mann often wandered off into the field during a sunset to feel at peace. She would often take pictures and meditate on the memory of her daughter. She took out her Samsung and showed me a sunset picture of the field with yellow flowers. I told her that she should continue going there if it brought her peace.

The front door opened and the coffee folks returned. Officer Mann asked how the session went and his wife gave him a quick rundown, emphasizing their daughter's presence. Mrs. Mann asked me if she could hug me, which I did. Then, I shook hands and hugged Officer Mann. They both left the house feeling refreshed and at peace. I'm sure they had a lot to talk about in the car on the way home.

As for me, I felt amazed...and incredibly hungry.

Meet the Clair Sisters!

While the words "clairvoyant" and "clairvoyance" are casually tossed around to indicate any kind of psychic and psychic ability, technically, clairvoyance is more of a specific function that can be used to see into not only the future, but the past and present.

"How do you receive information? Do you actually see things?" This is a common question I get. Hollywood/TV/Movies don't really help in that things don't necessarily appear in IMAX glory, complete with tense orchestral music. So, I introduce people to the Five "Clair" Sisters (and their weird cousin, also named "Clair")

Clairvoyance (clear seeing) – When you see information through your mind's eye. It can feel like deep imagination. Sight can be subjective or objective. Images can be literal or symbolic.

Clairaudience (clear hearing) – When you hear information. Hearing can be objective or subjective. Not to be confused with 5150's [the mentally unstable] hearing voices. Joan of Arc was probably clairaudient.

Clairsentience (clear sensing/feeling) – When you feel information. Some cops and detectives use clairsentience. "This doesn't feel right." "I'm getting a strong hunch – a gut feeling…" Clairsentience can also be feeling in your own body what a spirit experienced while alive. For example, when my chest hurts, the spirit probably had a heart attack. A sharp pain in my stomach could mean that the spirit passed from abdominal issues (stabbing, shooting, appendicitis, etc.)

Clairgustance and **Clairaliance** (clear tasting and clear smelling) – Psychic tasting and smelling. For example, I was describing a woman to a sitter whom felt like it was her dead mother. Suddenly, I smelled cleaning products with lemon-scented additives, and Pine-Sol. The sitter said it was her Mom, who always used those cleaning products. During a séance, a spicy food taste would appear in my mouth, which had nothing to do with my last meal. Turns out it was the spirit's favorite food while alive.

That Weird Cousin, **Claircognizance** (clear knowing) – You don't "see/hear/sense/taste/smell" the information. Instead, it's all downloaded into your brain in an instant, and you just "know." You don't know how you know—you just KNOW.

Now, you put it all together using sometimes more than one Clair [see Chapter 8].

CHAPTER EIGHT

Doesn't Everyone Love a Parade?

When: Sunday, July 7th

Where: Platform at the Spiritualist Church

Me: "To the woman sitting at the aisle, third row back, may I please approach you?"

Woman: [She stood up at her seat and remained standing] "Thank you, Russell. My name is Dina." Dina appears to be a woman in her late 50's.

Me: "Good morning, Dina. As I step into your vibration, I am picking up a gentleman coming from behind you. There is much fanfare about him. It's like he's blowing a trumpet or trombone to announce his arrival.

"He has a round head with a ruddy complexion, and he is large both in height and girth. His hair is thinning and he has a mustache. I'm feeling something in my chest, so he probably passed away from a heart problem.

"The energy I get from him is one of fatherly energy. If he isn't your actual Dad, then he has a paternal approach to you. Anyway, the message I am getting from him is for you to be out in the public, like a baton twirler at a parade.

"I see you going down a parade route as if you were leading it. Occasionally, you turn around to see how everyone is doing, and they continue to follow. Perhaps this is symbolic of you needing to lead by example. Don't worry about the people 'behind you.' They will catch up when it's time for them to catch up with you. Just smile and keep the parade going!

"Anyway, I don't know if this made any sense to you, but I will leave you with Blessings from Spirit."

Dina: "Russell, that was my father you described, with his complexion, size, and how he died. He had a strong presence when he walked into a room. Did you know that I'm actually going to be in a parade??"

Me: "What? No…"

Dina: "I'm going to be in the Sierra Madre community parade. [sounds of people gasping in the congregation] I will be driving a red convertible with some elderly dignitaries sitting on the trunk, with their feet on the back seat. I will have to look behind me every now and then to make sure they don't fall off the back!"

Me: "Well, thank you for confirming that information, Dina! Would you fill out an affidavit for me?" [chuckles in the congregation]

Sunday, July 15th, on the Platform at the Spiritualist Church

It's one thing to give spirit greetings/readings to random people in the congregation. But to give one to a certified medium, reverend, and speaker is something else…

Me: "Reverend Ernest Leard, may I please approach you with a message from Spirit?" ["Ernie" is seated in the very back row and is in his mid-60's. He and his family moved from Virginia and he and his wife currently live in Orange County, CA. Ernie has been gently pushing me to make sure my homework assignments get done, that my paperwork is in order, and that I haven't fallen behind. He really would like to see me as a speaker and a certified minister as well, but I'm perfectly happy working towards my certification as a clairvoyant medium].

Ernest: "Yes, Russell, thanks." [He stands up]

Me: "As I approach your vibration, a gentleman is stepping behind you and placing his hand on your shoulder in close friendship. He is dressed in what appears to be a U.S. Navy uniform. Underneath his clothes, next to his dog tags, I see multiple chains and cords around his neck in which he wears various lucky charms and spiritual symbols from his travels.

"He leans in close to you and laughs private, insider laughs, like you both have shared in adventures and funny tales. This man passed from hemorrhaging—like he popped a blood vessel—I'm seeing blood leaking out.

"He brings you a gift. It's a Japanese lucky cat figurine that sits by the front door. One of its paws moves back and forth, either by battery, or some rocking motion, indicating that the cat is "waving in" prosperity and new energy. Perhaps he saw this if/when he visited Japan? I don't know...either way, I will bless you and leave you that message from Spirit."

After the service was done, Ernest turned in a mediumship affidavit. That man I described was a close friend from the Navy who passed from hemorrhaging. I described him well. They had both spent some time in Japan together.

Giving a message to Reverend Ernest Leard was a good lesson in putting aside one's ego. Our ego is afraid of being judged by someone in authority. While people with titles, education and more experience should be given respect, the truth is that whether a person is the President or a peasant, they have the same needs as everyone else. The spirits wish to communicate with them and to send them love and healing, just as our guides wish to do the same for us.

Filtering Out Your Imagination By Being Inside Your Imagination

One major concern new students of mediumship might have is whether what you are receiving might be just your imagination, versus what might be legitimate outside information from Spirit.
I discovered one technique which helps and that is to be inside your imagination, first. It's a way of "distracting" your imagination by keeping it busy enough to allow the psychic information to sneak through.
Instead of just waiting for the spiritual-psychic information to simply appear in your head, it might be easier to put yourself into an imaginary state, first. You can imagine yourself sitting in front of a large TV screen, perhaps in an expensive, private theater, with lovely, adjustable seats. Imagine the information appearing on the big screen. If you are introducing a spirit to a sitter, perhaps imagine the spirit walking onto a stage where there's a standing microphone in the middle, but the stage is in darkness. Suddenly, a spotlight would

appear at the spirit's feet, with the spotlight growing bigger in diameter, revealing the spirit's legs and clothing, and finally revealing the entire person. Imagine the person stepping up close to the microphone and speaking into it.

When facilitating development classes, I have had student successes when I would talk the student into imagining that they were in another place waiting for the information to either appear or to be heard.

Chapter Nine

Practicing Advance Clairvoyance Deliberately

Sometimes, you can't always be a part of a development circle. The next best thing to do, though frowned upon by some mediumship teachers, is to try your hand at advance clairvoyance.

Time frame: Wednesday night, October 23 to Thursday morning, October 24, 2019

Dear Readers,

Happy Halloween Season!

Since I've been practicing "live mediumship" versus "advance clairvoyance," I haven't been a human psychic answering machine in a while. Still, it's nice to practice advance clairvoyance if one is unable to give a one-on-one reading. And, practicing ANY of the psychic senses is a good thing because it can only aide in mediumship development.

I was meditating at my ancestor/spirit altar [technically, an altar is not needed to be a medium, but I wanted to set one up as part of my Chinese heritage] on Wednesday evening, when I opened up and asked, "Is there anyone here for anyone that I know?"

I immediately received an image of an employee in Detective Bureau. Well, I knew this detective wasn't dead because I just saw her yesterday and I didn't feel anything bad around her. So, I figured this detective was the "recipient." So, I asked for the spirit attached to this detective. I tried to remember all the information I was shown, but I was also very tired. As fun as Civilian Appreciation Day was at LAPD Headquarters, it was still a long work day.

The next morning...

OK, I have to call this detective who has no clue that I'm "doing this stuff." Back out on a limb. We connected on the phone and I relayed the following information:

A grandmother or grand aunt, possibly on Mom's side of the family.

You have a black and white portrait photo of her. She has wavy hair, wears or owns pearls (earrings, necklace), may appear feminine, but was as tough as nails. No-nonsense personality.

She is walking with you (or another grand sibling) on the sidewalk. There are cypress trees nearby, or on her property, or she lived in Cypress [when you only receive visual/clairvoyant information, you have to sometimes guess if the symbol is literal, like actual cypress trees, or maybe it's the name of a city, or could be a symbol].

I don't see her as a formal teacher, like a paid school classroom teacher. Instead, she has a gift for teaching people as a hobby, like teaching adults how to sew.

The name "Marilyn" comes up. Or any name that has the sound of "M-L-N" like "Marlene" or "Melanie" or "Melana." But, this is not her name – probably someone that the both of you know.

I then shared a personal message from this spirit, and asked that I don't be called "nutty-cuckoo" by the detective!

The detective then shared that I was referring to the paternal grandmother (I am still practicing mom/dad 's side). The spirit fit the photo description and the personality.

The detective didn't mention anything about Cypress or cypress trees, but chuckled when I mentioned teaching sewing. The grandmother never had a real job. Grandfather worked and took care of her. But later, this grandmother ended up teaching (as a hobby) adults how to use a sewing machine.

The name "Marilyn" made sense because this was grandmother's best friend, whom the detective also knew very well.

The detective thanked me for opening up, stepping up, and passing along this information. As it turns out, after the birth of the detective's first child (a son), the detective was having recurring dreams of BOTH grandmothers visiting their great-grandson. And, since I happened to know the detective, perhaps I was the closest and nearest "answering service" available. I was the confirmation for the detective's dreams.

May you be blessed by your Ancestors this Hallow's Eve!

What is the mediumship certification process like?

Between 2017 to when I passed my exams, the process was a logistical complication that required patience. I heard that some changes were underway to make it logistically easier.

First, the NSAC doesn't certify "itinerant mediums." You have to be a member of a NSAC church or camp and be serving their platform for so many years. When you apply for the steps to become ultimately certified, you are given a 5 year limitation, along with certain time restraints between certain steps. For example, you have to be a member of a church or camp for at least 2 years before applying for the final exams.

The MPI mailed me a thick notebook. There was much reading and writing of essays and I was assigned an advisor who would grade my material and make comments. Mine was a reverend on the East Coast of the United States named Sharon. My first papers were sent through regular mail, then the rest were emailed to Sharon. I was able to complete this in about 6 months.

For practicum, the NSAC headquarters located in Lily Dale, New York (an entire town dedicated to Spiritualism) required for me to submit at least 6 "Mental Mediumship Affidavits" written by people in the congregation explaining that my demonstration of mediumship was the real deal on a personal level. Affidavits were kept in the back of the church, and before my public demonstration, the chairperson announced that I was a student working towards certification and that if anyone felt that my message was accurate enough, to please fill one out and hand it to a church board member.

The affidavit itself required the sitter's name, address, and phone number, followed by the name of the medium giving the message and the date received. It had a three-lined blank section asking that the sitter explain briefly how the message I gave was relevant to me bringing forth evidence to the sitter of their deceased loved one. There were also boxes to be checked off by the sitter mentioning things like:

• Name
• Description
• Method of passing
• Where lived
• Character
• Shared memories
• Relationship
• Personality
• Knowledge of recent events [known only to the sitter]
• Age
• Health conditions

The sitter would sign the affidavit, and then it had to be signed by 2 witnesses, specifically church workers present on that day.

So, an affidavit couldn't be accepted from a one-on-one reading in private, but in front of the public at a church service or church-sponsored platform demonstration, with at least two church workers (board member, another certified medium, secretary, minister, etc.) present.

To make it a little harder, it was certainly possible to receive 2 or more affidavits from the same person over a period of time, but we could only submit one affidavit per sitter. Just pick the one that looked more impressive. Also, one of the affidavits had to be from the same year that the student was applying for the final exam.

I'm not sure of the reason for this requirement. Maybe to prevent the medium from becoming complacent after s/he has gathered 6 or more affidavits in their earlier years? To keep student mediums on their toes?

Reverend Ernest Leard told me to submit 12 instead of 6. He explained that during the review of the affidavits, some might be rejected because of various reasons. Some sitters just can't write or fill out a basic form. Some sitters glowed with how psychic the medium was able to clairvoyantly reveal information, but the affidavit is asking for details of mediumship, not being psychic. Turning in 12 provided back up in case a few affidavits were not good enough (I turned in my best 12). COVID did not help because the church was closed for over a year. After reopening, I was able to apply for my two final exams. One was open book and had to be completed in about 45 days from the time I received it in the mail.

The second exam was closed book and had to be taken in front of 3 proctors who were members of the church or working in the NSAC. It was decided that the easiest way to do this was to hold my test inside the church after a Sunday service. People were encouraged to move their socializing to the parking lot or a local coffee shop, then the church doors were locked. My exam was pulled from an envelope and I was given a pen. It took me about 2.5 hours to complete it, without hesitation or breaks. My hand was hurting. The exam was placed in an envelope which was then sealed. I had to write my signature across the envelope seal. Then, that envelope was placed in another envelope for one of the proctors to mail off.

After waiting, I was told that I passed, but not told how I did on the test or what I got incorrect.

Finally, a Sunday was chosen in October of 2021 in which I was called up to the platform and presented my certificate suitable for framing. There was also cake and refreshments waiting after the church service in honor of my accomplishments.

CHAPTER TEN

You Invited Them to Dinner?

Sometimes when doing mediumship, a relative might step forth who wasn't exactly close to the sitter. But, you're not here to judge because you're just the telephone.

Dear Readers,

Happy Holiday Season!

Pumpkin pies, autumn leaves, festive gatherings, cooler weather, lights, songs & cider with your loved ones...

Wait a second...

You don't like being around that creepy uncle? -that cousin on your Mom's side is always trying to out-boast you? -your father was always so distant?

Let's face it. They may be family members, but sometimes we might feel closer to our best friends than our own blood. Holidays are those awkward times when we reunite with those relatives we wouldn't normally see any other time of the year.

Just because someone doesn't have a physical body doesn't make it any less awkward.

Some months ago, I had a father in spirit show up for his daughter in the congregation. He felt like "dad energy" but he kept switching positions behind the sitter, so that I had trouble determining whether he was indeed her father, or merely a "father-figure" or an uncle. [In a previous journal entry] If you remember, the sitter later confirmed that it was her father, but that he had an unstable relationship with his daughter which was never resolved on his death bed. So, she felt that this man who was biologically her parent was never truly deserving of the title of the role of "Father." That probably explained why her father would not firmly stand behind the daughter's left shoulder to take his position as "Dad."

Mediumship communication is a lot about symbols. The medium and the spirits teach each other and help each other to solve the puzzles. I think if you were ever good at playing charades, or giving those secret hand signals in a baseball or football game, that it might make mediumship easier.

With the next example, I feel that Spirit is trying to teach me (again) what it's like to communicate with a "shifty relative" just like the above example with the distant father.

When: Sunday, October 27, 2019

Where: Spiritualist Church of Revelation, Monrovia, California – On Platform

I asked permission if I could give a message to the lady in the second row, next to the aisle.

Her name was "Patsy" and she told me, "OK."

"As we step into your vibration, I am picking up a man who feels like an uncle to you. But it's hard to say whether he is a blood uncle, or a man known by your parents whom you would refer to as an uncle…"

Why didn't this "uncle" guy stand still? Usually, they stand on one side or the other of the sitter. This guy kinda' shuffled here and there, until finally Patsy's dead father took him by the arm and made him stand still for a while. Some of us are familiar already with Patsy's dead Dad. He has come through before, and this felt like her father "dragging" this uncle into the spotlight.

This guy had a grin on his face that said, "OK, you caught me! But, aren't I fun?! Let's get a drink!" I explained that this odd uncle felt less organized or less disciplined than her father. He was inclined to have a good time, play music, without any desire to be tied down with responsibilities and commitments. He also shared with me a word to give to Patsy. The word was "sugar." I didn't know if this was a term of endearment, or that he gave her sweets. He apologized for not keeping various promises.

Later, Patsy filled out an affidavit for me. She explained that the spirit was her Uncle Charlie, who sometimes went by "Uncle Chuck." Yes, he was a blood uncle – the brother of her father. He was hedonistic and never took his uncle role very seriously. No wonder her dead dad had to drag Uncle Charlie into the spotlight.

Now, it made sense to me. In reference to the previous female sitter who never made peace with her difficult father, his spirit never stood still behind her left shoulder because his role as a father was questionable.

I am slowly learning spirit sign-language.

The word "sugar" was an easy one for Patsy. She was battling a recent diagnosis: Type II Diabetes. "Sugar" was the warning from this uncle, who was now wanting to apologize for his half-hearted involvement with his surviving niece.

"Robin, may I…"

"Yes, Russell! I knew that you would be giving me the message!" [Board member Robin Quiroz always enjoys receiving messages from me.]

"OK! As we step into your vibration, what's odd for today is that I feel I'm getting the messages first, and then I need to ask whom it's coming from. So, the first thing I am seeing are scarecrows. You have a bunch of scarecrows. [I've never been to Robin's home in Apple Valley, but I saw scarecrow imagery in my mind.

The day after, Robin sent me a bunch of photos of scarecrows on her property as confirmation]. The scarecrows are also symbolic to me. They represent being present to show that you mean business, but without having to take physical action. Just showing others that you are standing on-guard means that you are being vigilant, without having to resort to extreme measures or force."

Robin nodded her head emphatically. It felt like this confirmation might have something to do with boundary issues with difficult relatives. But, I continued...

"The man who is sending me this image stands behind your left shoulder, but older than Dad. His height is similar to Reverend Ernest Leard's height, and so is his build. He is wearing denim, like overalls."

"That's my grandfather, Russell," Robin replied. "And those are his denim overalls he liked to work in."

Whew! At least Grandpa stood still behind Robin's shoulders!

CHAPTER ELEVEN

The "Myth" of Halloween; Pushing Too Hard

It's common among popular folklore that séances are best conducted near or on Halloween, because somehow the "veil is thinner" during this time in the Northern Hemisphere. As Spiritualists, we don't think so, for the simple reason that we feel the spirit realm is not affected by a small planet's orbit around the sun, no matter how much folklore and ritualistic practice is assigned to this phenomenon.

But, since we are humans who participate in culture, it is natural for us to want to ascribe paranormal things to certain observations in nature, and spirits do have the ability to influence the natural world to some degree, too.

Whether you are someone who prefers assigning meaning to weather patterns, the flight of birds, thunderstorms, etc., it helps to also be open to Spirit contact beyond our cultural expectations, too.

Another lesson in mediumship is that it should be done with "alert relaxation." Don't push too hard. The following blog entry which occurred close to Halloween demonstrates this.

Dear Readers,

So, I was asked to give a sermon for Sunday, October 6th, since the church could not find another speaker. Any topic.

Hmmm…

Something about Halloween.

I called upon my ancient powers of anthropological thinking to come aid me. I also brought along a big witch's hat, and a khaki-colored pith helmet. I discussed:

The Celtic festival of summer's end, called "Samhain" (pronounced: SAH-when, an Irish word for the end of summer), and how Samhain is also the Celtic New Year on October 31st. Thank the Celts for Halloween.

- Jack o'Lanterns were originally carved from turnips, because pumpkins were from the New World. When the Irish and Scottish immigrated to America, they discovered the pumpkin, fell in love with it over the turnip, and so America switched over to carving pumpkins, thanks to the Irish and Scots (two of the seven Celtic nations).

- The Catholic Church superimposed All Saints' Day and All Souls' Day over the festival practices of Samhain. All Hallow's

Eve is actually a Christian term (Halloween) for a pagan holiday (Samhain).

- Whatever you wish to call it, it's a time to think about, and contact, our beloved Dead. It is believed that this is the time to especially do it.

- As Spiritualists, we don't need a "season for a séance." For example, we don't need Thanksgiving Day to give thanks and express our gratitude all year round.

- But, sometimes having a special holiday as a reminder is a nice thing to celebrate. Give thanks always, but eat your turkey on Thanksgiving. Likewise, feel free to commune with the Dead outside of Halloween.

When I talked about Halloween, I wore the witch's black, pointy hat. And, when I talked about anthropological theories, I took off the witch hat and put on my explorer's pith helmet. I'm a man of many hats.

When it was time to work the Platform, I did something I should not have done: push too hard. I was hoping that I would try to use ALL my "clairs" for each person. Clairvoyance, clairaudience, clairsentience, etc., etc. Well, you don't just "expect" it all to show up like that. Later, Rev. Ernest Leard told me to next time just "invite" the information to show up in the best way possible, and use your strongest "clairs." Spirit usually works with our best "clairs" to get messages through. It takes a lot of work, and since Spirit doesn't like to waste energy, they want to get messages through in the easiest and best ways possible, versus the medium's ego attempting to prove something.

So, I would start out my messages explaining things that I saw and felt, but when I attempted to go into the other "clairs," people looked at me funny.

During development class after church, I was practicing on Robin. I was describing a man to her, whom she just wasn't connecting with. Interestingly, Reverend Ernest Leard also saw him, and included his working environment, which I also saw. After a while, I realized that the man was bugging Robin to let her know that he was associated with a female relative of hers. I guess the spirit didn't want to talk to Robin – he wanted Robin to talk to his loved one who is still alive.

Silently, I begged,"OK, Spirit...don't you have anything substantial to bring through? I feel like I am floundering."

Suddenly, I saw a waitress on roller skates, carrying a tray with an ice cream sundae, or milk shake.

"Robin, do you know anyone in spirit who was a waitress on roller skates?"

"No, Russell, I can't think of any deceased relatives on roller skates..."

"Well, perhaps she wasn't a waitress? Maybe she was a telephone operator supervisor from the 1930's? They wore roller skates when they had to continually move back and forth between switchboards. Or, perhaps a secretary working in Congress...they had to wear skates just to go back and forth in that large building from office to office. Anyone at all??"

Sometimes, mediumship is frustrating.

Robin continued to look at me as if I were nuts. Well, that's common. Most people think that anyone claiming to be a medium is nutsy-cuckoo. And, sometimes being Russell Chan means being a little bit nutsy-cuckoo.

"Well, Russell, my daughter was once a waitress at a Sonic Drive-In restaurant. She served customers on roller skates..."

Geesh. Happy Halloween!

Apologies to the other ancient cultures...Chapter 11 simply covered a particular day at the church in which I gave my sermon about the origins of Halloween. Since I am an unofficial "Celtophile" who had a limited amount of time for my sermon, I only covered Ireland's contribution to the holiday, versus the ancient Romans, Egyptians, etc.

CHAPTER TWELVE

The Difference Between a Psychic Reading Vs. Mediumship

The NSAC does not allow the use of occult tools in their practice. Keep your crystal balls, Tarot cards, pendulums, oils, astrology charts, and stones at home. Also, a psychic reading is all about the client (their wishes, dreams, problems, relationships, finances, career, etc.), while a mediumship reading (or "sitting") is more about identifying a deceased loved one with evidence. Now, the spirit can certainly give their ghostly opinion about the client's current life, but the emphasis is on triangular communication.

However, when we are "off duty" with the NSAC and not officially representing the church as a Spiritualist medium, that's our own personal business. Many Spiritualist mediums still enjoy collecting occult paraphernalia just because they like these items, find them fun to collect, or use them outside of mediumship. I own over 30 decks of Tarot cards and many crystal balls, but I never use them when practicing mediumship or when representing the NSAC. Come to think of it, I've almost never used any crystal balls in my home. They are mostly for decoration.

So, if you are conducting a psychic reading, stressing that it's NOT mediumship, you can divine the cracks in a ceiling for all we care (yes, a good psychic can do that).

But, the Universe is way beyond our little human powers of compartmentalization, as you will soon read...

When: One evening before the 2019 Thanksgiving Holiday

The text on my mobile read something like, "I'm at my son's Taekwondo studio. We live just a few mins from home. When we get home, I'll call you."

Oh great, it's "get ready, get set... cool your heels," I thought. I was hoping that the West Traffic Division (WTD) police officer would be ready for her telephone reading at the given time, so I had meditated and prepared myself in my living room, with a deck of Tarot cards sitting in front of me...and she had to get home, first.

Three Months Earlier, In August...

I was visiting a Tip-A-Cop event at Wood Ranch BBQ at The Grove in August. Tip-A-Cop is a local fundraiser in which police officers become serving staff at a local participating restaurant. Any tips the cops raise go to the Special Olympics.

One of my WTD cop friends introduced me to some of her fellow sworn. I remember giving my phone number out, but didn't remember much of anything after that, except that I got to meet the brother of a sergeant in Office of Operations.

The officer who received my phone number texted me in November, asking for a reading. Due to logistics and distance, she paid The Green Man Store, and the store then notified me that this client wanted to schedule a session. The day and the time would be between the two of us, since I was not required to drive down to the store to use their telephones.

I had explained to her in a previous text that it would be strictly a Tarot card reading, as I generally do not mix mediumship with psychic readings. Many people go to see a psychic with issues that have nothing to do with dead loved ones. So, now I had to sit and wait for her and her son to return home. I didn't want to get up and watch TV, prepare dinner, browse Facebook, or do anything that would take me out of my "mode". So, I just sat at my altar and relaxed...

Oops! Some spirit came to visit!

I silently explained to any spirits that I was about to do a reading for someone, and that just because I "opened myself" to the spiritual realms, it didn't mean that I was an open phone booth. I politely commanded that anyone *not* connected to this client to please leave immediately.

The spirit remained.

Her hair was above shoulder length, dirty blonde, and naturally frizzy. Unlike the cop who was dark/Latina, this female spirit appeared light-skinned Caucasian, had pale eyes, and looked naturally-pretty when not wearing makeup. She had a few freckles but was not a red-head. I got the feeling that she had died young. I had a vision of her on her death bed, her face/head so swollen and discolored, that she was unrecognizable. I didn't receive the cause of her death, except that it did not feel like an accident or foul play.

When I asked her how she was related to the cop, the spirit stood on the right side of the cop (in my mind), which indicated that the spirit was at least known by the cop's mother. However, the spirit stood to the side of the cop and away from her. That meant that she was a peer, like a friend, cousin, or co-worker [ancestors stand behind the sitter's shoulders].

The message she gave to me was the cutting motion made with both hands sweeping left and right, like a referee signing No Play, or Missed Field Goal. But, instead of it being a sports signal, the motion intuitively said to me to tell the officer to "cut it out." The bad habit I felt was not inherently harmful (like an addiction), but more like a way of thinking and communicating that proved that this officer's greatest enemy was her own self. She could be the one who cut off her own success.

This self-sabotage was confirmed later in the Tarot card spread, when "The Devil" card appeared.

After I gave her the card reading, she told me that I was 100% right about everything, and she proceeded to do a breakdown of the reading with supporting details.

Great! If the card reading resonated with her, I felt then that I could give her the surprise icing on the cake.

I told her about the female spirit that showed up while I was waiting for her and her son to arrive home from his martial arts lesson. She almost started to choke up. It was her friend who had died of cancer. The physical descriptions matched, and on her death bed, her face/head was unrecognizable due to swelling and discoloration. And the message made sense, since the cards (and the cop) confirmed it. What freaked her out was that as soon as I mentioned the spirit's presence, an air filter in her home that was pre-set to turn on and off at specific times nowhere near the time of the reading, had a mysterious electrical surge or "hiccup".

"Yes," I reassured her, "they can do that. It's a way of saying Hello."

After Thanksgiving, my friend called me to say that her co-worker was impressed. I was just grateful that my Guides were able to bring forth the spirit of the cop's young friend.

Can Spirits Give Psychic Readings?

Yes, absolutely.
The primary job of an evidential medium is to bring forth facts and messages from the Dead Person to the living sitter. Those facts are usually details about the Dead Person and any information that is known in between the sitter and the Dead. The medium is not supposed to go off into "fortune telling."
But, sometimes a spirit will give information that seems more like a psychic reading to the sitter. My personal advice is to treat this information as just as valid or invalid if you were receiving it from a live psychic. Just because a being is in the spirit world does not mean that they will be 100% accurate. Being invisible does not grant one the power of knowing everything in the universe.
I remember one Sunday morning when Reverend Ernest Leard was on platform. He was giving a message to my boyfriend, Jim. Part of the message included the spirit telling Jim to be aware of his engine light going on and to have it fixed as soon as possible. The next morning on his way to work, Jim's engine light went on. He could feel the engine

responding in a dysfunctional manner and immediately drove to his dealership where a serious problem was diagnosed. Thank you, spirit!

CHAPTER THIRTEEN

A Preamble is Helpful, and Spirits Can Work with Artifacts

Sometimes, thanks to movies and fiction, people have odd expectations when consulting with mediums. A preamble is useful because it clears things up. If doing a private session, you can email or text a preamble to the sitter before the session. I've included my own in Appendix II.

Besides revealing details about their former lives on earth, spirits can also send the medium "artifacts." The spirits can see what's happening to their loved ones on earth. They can mention to the medium that the sitter just painted their kitchen a ghastly burgundy color, remind the sitter of a gift or token that the spirit had given to them when they were alive, or they can reveal the contents of the sitter's purse, just to prove that they are still around and watching out for us.

If you are asking a spirit for evidence, besides the usual questions of how they died and what job or hobbies they had while alive, you can ask the spirit to reveal artifacts.

The following blog entry was written on Monday, August 5, 2019 from the Sunday before.

Dear Readers,

When: Sunday, August 4, 2019, Spiritualist Church of Revelation, Monrovia, CA

It had been three weeks since I had been to church and I felt rusty. Would the spirits still talk to me? Did I lose my abilities? Aren't mediums allowed to go on vacation?

But it wasn't like I was shirking. Even though I hadn't been to church in weeks, I was meditating at home, using the technique called "Sitting in the Power". This meditative technique was "invented" by a Scottish medium, became popular in the UK, and finally made its way to the USA. It's sometimes called "Sitting in the Silence" or "Sitting for Spirit." Although I have not checked yet, I believe YouTube might have a few videos explaining how to meditate this way.

When Mike M. and I took the Platform, we noticed some new faces in the congregation. I decided that I would give them my "preamble". Besides explaining stuff to the new folks, sometimes giving a preamble actually "awakens" the medium that they are "ready" to receive information.

In my preamble, I welcomed the new people to the church. I explained briefly that Mike M. and I were both student mediums, still working on our certifications. I told them that in my world travels, I have witnessed mediumship in different cultures and religions.

For example, I explained that while in Singapore, the Chinese mediums practiced in Buddhist and Taoist temples. There would be loud music, with banging gongs and drums. There would be tranced dancing, along with self-mutilation, the drawing of charms and prayers on paper with blood taken from the medium's sliced tongue, and messages uttered forth from Buddhist deities. The place would be covered in incense and candles. The shrines would be adorned with fresh fruits.

Next, I shared my experience of visiting northern Brazil and how I witnessed mediumship being practiced in the religion of Umbanda (the Brazilian cousin of Voudun and Santeria). I told them that chickens were sacrificed, people would fall into trance while dancing to the beat of West African drums, the priest and priestess would blow cigar smoke and spray cachaça (Brazilian rum) between their teeth, spraying the participants, and beaded necklaces would be blessed by the spirits possessing the dancers. The languages spoken would be a combination of West African languages (mostly Yoruban) and Brazilian Portuguese.

But, we are in America. And, modern Spiritualism as practiced in the USA/UK/Canada doesn't involve any of these things. Mike M. humorously added that just a few days ago, we had the church carpet shampooed, so we were grateful that we did not have to deal with sacrificial blood (which would be difficult to remove). Instead, one of the mediums would call on a person in the congregation. The person chosen would need to give his/her permission to receive a message, because the mediums don't "push messages" onto people without their permission. Then, the person should stand (if they can stand, because a lot of people are very old and cannot stand easily). After standing, the person should say their first name out loud.

The medium would then give a message or greeting from the spirit world. No, it's not a psychic reading – we won't reveal winning lottery numbers or your next love interest. I explained that sometimes things might not make sense. While we certainly could be wrong (mediumship, like meteorology and stock-market analysis, is never perfect), it's a good idea to keep the information tucked away. Sometimes, evidence will re-surface later. I also explained that we were not "sorcerers" who could conjure up the spirit of anyone. Sometimes, the dead person you really want to connect with might not come through, but someone else might show up from your history.

After giving the preamble, I was beginning to sweat on the Platform. Jim later confirmed that it was me, and not the warmth in the room because the room temperature was comfortable. I felt fidgety and somehow "heightened."

At the end of the church service, I had three people who wanted my business card and asked if I did any spiritual work outside of the church.

"Ma'am, may I approach you, please?" There was a woman in the second row whom I've never seen at the church, She looked to be about late 40's or early 50's. She was attractive, had reddish-brown hair, pale skin, vibrant blue eyes, and a nice figure. She looked fashionably put-together.

"Yes, thank you, Russell," she answered and stood up. In this blog, I call her "Tina."

"Tina, as we step into your vibration, I want to say....Aloha! Greetings from the Hawaiian islands! I am sensing a man standing very close to you. He is very protective. He is wearing a green leaf crown, flowers wrapped around his wrists and ankles, and a grass skirt or sarong. He looks to be in his early 30's. Now, unless you just lost a Polynesian boyfriend who liked to hula dance, I am feeling that perhaps this might be a spirit guide.

He is showing me that you have been acting rather carelessly and putting yourself into dangerous situations. No, not sky-diving danger, but more like walking across an empty parking lot in the dark, in a bad neighborhood, unaware of your surroundings. He is showing me that you have the inner demeanor of a Hell's Angels biker dude. But Tina, in this life you were born into the body of a thin female with delicate features. You are not a Biker Dude. This guide is saying to just please be careful and aware. And with that, I will leave you with Blessings from Spirit."

Tina approached me after the church service to thank me for the message. Tina said that she lived in Hawaii for a few months and that she needed to be more aware of her surroundings. She had purposely put herself into situations that many people would normally avoid, by working with the homeless, with drug addicts, and having also associated with biker gangs. She had an open airline ticket to return to Hawaii and was wondering when she would use it. She would now consider possibly returning, once her financial affairs were in order.

"Robin, may I approach you, please?" Robin Quiroz is one of the spiritual healers and administrative workers and board members at the church. She is quite talented at PK (psychokinesis – the influencing of matter through thought, like bending spoons). She has never been interested in becoming a mental medium and prefers to stick with energy healing.

Spirit congratulated her with having some toxic family members finally move out of her home, and to make sure that the void was not filled with similar energies. The spirits giving the message were a "cowboy" and her mother.

Suddenly, I saw a toy that I have at home. When Spirit sometimes wants to show me something about someone, they will choose something from my "databank." In this case, it was a small Loch Ness Monster plushie – a green smiling monster wearing a Tam O' Shanter on its head. I picked it up while I was visiting Edinburgh, Scotland.

So, I told Robin, "You can continue cleaning out your home, but Spirit is telling you that it's OK to keep the little green dragon. Don't throw it out."

Robin looked puzzled. She didn't know what I was talking about.

"It could be a plush-toy, or a figurine, of a green dragon, or a green reptile. If I really had to stretch it, I'd say perhaps a green jade pendant of a dragon or serpent? Either way, just keep it. It doesn't take up any room. And with that, I will leave you with Blessings from Spirit."

It wasn't until Monday morning that Robin confirmed what I was being shown. It was a chew toy that her two dogs enjoyed. I think it's an alligator or crocodile toy. Still, it is an object much appreciated – by her dogs!

Focus In For Details

If you are clairvoyantly receiving an artifact, but it's not clear enough or hazy, ask Spirit to give further details. You are allowed to ask for clarification! You can also imagine that you are looking at the object through a spy camera lens which can zero in onto specific details of the object.
If the sitter can confirm the object, ask if it isn't too much effort to send you a picture of it.

- In Chapter 13, Robin volunteered a picture of her dog's chew toy on Monday morning which matched my description.

- I was giving a test reading to one of the owners of The Green Man Store. While on the phone, I was describing a lime-green dress belonging to the store owner's mother in spirit, along with matching green jewelry. She was able to text me a photo of her mother wearing the dress and jewelry while attending a wedding.

- While reading the same owner mentioned above, the spirit of a white, long-haired cat dashed out from under my altar where I was sitting and ran underneath my couch. "All right, who owned a white, fluffy cat? The cat-ghost just ran through my living room..."

"BLIZZARD!" exclaimed the woman over the phone. "You saw our cat, Blizzard!" She immediately texted me a photo of the white, long-haired cat.

CHAPTER FOURTEEN

20 Years Later!

Be careful what you say when doing any kind of reading for someone. You might just be "in the moment" but the sitter might remember it for years and years as the following blog shows.

Dear Reader,

Sometimes, a psychic/mediumistic reading confirmation is revealed immediately. Sometimes, it comes a few days later. And sometimes, you won't find out until MANY years later.

On Thursday evening, May 30, 2019, I was attending the retirement dinner for Devonshire Division's Detective Commanding Officer, whom I worked with in three different assignments.

While I was mingling, a Police Officer 3 (P-III, which is a rank below a Sergeant) approached me and gave me a hug. I hadn't seen this officer in a very long time. She said that while people tell her things, she forgot a lot of things, but she always remembered what I told her.

What did I tell her? I can barely remember what I've said. She said that when I was working for the Van Nuys Public Library (next door to LAPD Van Nuys Area Station), she sometimes came to the library to say hello to the staff. She said that one day, I was holding her hand, looking past her as if I was gazing far away. I told her that she would become pregnant with a third child, and to be careful – something bad was going to happen to either her or someone she loved, involving LAPD.

That was over 20 years ago.

After I left the Library Department to join LAPD Foothill Division, she became pregnant with child number three. During her pregnancy, the Rampart Scandals was under investigation. She vividly remembered her husband and her being woken in the middle of the night by SWAT, raiding the inside of their house. She remembered sitting on her front porch, dressed in her nightgown, with her face in her hands, wondering what possibly had gone wrong. Her husband (also an officer) was in his underwear being interrogated. Her husband eventually left the force. She eventually divorced him and changed her last name. It seemed ages ago.

A Simple Yet Complex Response to Manifesting; Conquering Your Fears

This entry has a little lesson on manifesting. As a medium, you can help others, but it's OK to also help yourself. And when it comes to conquering your fears, it seems that the same advice in the "outside" world will also apply to mediumship development.

Dear Readers,

When: Sunday, November 27, 2022

Mediumship Development Class was canceled after church service because they wanted Jim and me to put up the church's Christmas tree.

My sermon that Sunday was on writing a letter to Santa Claus. I instructed the congregation that one should first send a holiday greeting, ask how Santa and the Missus were doing, how the reindeer were doing, and how the elves were doing. It's only polite. Then, go into what you wish for, whether it's intangibles (better relationships, peace on earth), and/or tangibles (new job, a car, etc.). Then, include the phrase "this or something better." You can sign it with your first name if you don't want to include your last name. Address the letter to Santa Claus at the North Pole. Add a stamp (or two). Do not include your return address because you don't want this letter returning to you.

"Are you telling me that your sermon was telling a bunch of adults how to write a letter to Santa Claus?"

Yes. But, it is a form of spiritual manifestation. When practicing magic of any kind, or even manifestation techniques under hypnosis or trance, it is important to reach the subconscious mind. You need to bypass the conscious mind which analyzes and criticizes. One method is to reach that state of "child-like innocence" that opens up the heart and a sense of wonder.

Also, from a cultural-anthropological perspective, people for thousands of years have written petitions to the spirit world. It could be to a saint, an ancestor, an angel, or a deity. The request is often "released" by burning the petition in a sacred flame, or folding it and placing it at a shrine or altar.

You cannot cast a successful spell when you are in the frame of mind that says, "I don't believe any of this." "This is stupid." "I'm an ADULT and I shouldn't believe in this nonsense." By writing a letter to Santa Claus, you need to suspend disbelief and the critical adult within. By writing down what you desire, you are also organizing your priorities and seeing it put on paper. By mailing the letter, you are releasing the desire which slips into the subconscious mind. It is the subconscious mind which actually runs your life and brings those "miracles" into your life.

By adding "this or something better," this allows your energy to reach for possibilities that are beyond your limited logic. It frees up the energy to bring you what you actually might need, versus the rigid form of what you desire. Always reach for the essence of something, versus the rigid form.

For example, say you want lots of money for a new wardrobe. But when you ask yourself why you need a new wardrobe, the answer might be because you want to gain new friends and you want to dress to impress to attract them. But on further inspection, what you really want are new friends. Why? Are you lonely? So, "this or something better" might not bring you cash, or maybe not even new clothes. What you really desire is companionship with the most compatible friends. True friends are not going to judge you based upon your attire. So, while the initial desire was for money for a new wardrobe, what you might actually manifest are situations in which you run into trustworthy, loyal, compatible people who end up being close friends.

I started writing a letter to Santa when I became an adult (not when I was a child). I haven't stopped since.

While on the platform...

There was a new face (pandemic-masked, but definitely someone new) sitting in the very back row.

I knew who it was because Michael Jose Zavala had been Facebook Messengering me about visiting the Spiritualist Church. He himself felt that he was a budding medium and was already doing psychic readings for others.

His background was in Wicca and Neo-Paganism, so I warned him ahead of time that Spiritualism was born during the Victorian Era – a church service will look a lot like a watered-down Christian service. People sit in rows facing a podium. Old, Victorian-era church hymns are sung, with some of the words changed to make it "less Christian." No drums, no bonfires, no animal masks, no ecstatic dancing, no food offerings to trees and rocks, no libations to Mother Earth. No hooded robes, no loincloths, no face paint, no ritual tools, no magic circles outlined with rocks. Still, Michael wanted to take an Uber and experience what a Spiritualist church service was like.

Other than that, I never met Michael, nor did I know his family or background. I was a little nervous at first because I knew that the other two mediums on platform were probably not going to pick on the "stranger" if they could help it. [Some mediums feel that] It's safer to give messages to known individuals.

When it was my time to speak, I explained to the congregation that I still felt like a student, and that I would prefer confirmation with either "Yes, no, or I don't know." Do not feed me any other information. I explained that getting "No" in a way helped me, because it helped me learn to focus and listen better to Spirit.

How do you face your fears? You address them head-on.

So, I picked on Michael in the last row. I explained to everyone that I like to pick on people in the last row because it ties the room together. It makes them feel more included. It also makes the speaker project their voice above the other heads to the back of the room. I learned about picking on people in the very last rows by books on platform and gallery mediumship. Makes sense to me.

Immediately, I saw an old man standing behind his right shoulder. He looked and felt like a grandfather (maternal side). He wore green/blue/gray plaid flannel and kept very quiet. But he had a wicked sense of humor, especially when one of the females in the family made a mistake or messed up. I explained to Michael that in his family (according to this grandfather figure), the women tended to be bossy and know-it-alls, and were efficient. So, when one of them messed up, he would chuckle to himself!

The message from this man was an odd one. "Keep trucking on." The image was of Michael in a pickup truck or truck, happily driving it.

Michael Zavala was able to confirm all of this. It was indeed his maternal grandfather, down to the clothes and humor. Also, his grandfather used to be a big-rig trucker. Michael himself would also end his psychic readings to his clients with "keep trucking on," meaning to keep moving forward.

Michael spoke to me while I was decorating the Christmas tree. He was glad that he visited the church and for receiving confirmation from his dead grandfather that he was on the right path as a medium.

I lit extra candles when I got home to thank my Guides for clarity and accuracy!

[While writing this book, I am proud to say that Michael Jose Zavala is currently working on his mediumship credentials through the MPI and has taken on more responsibilities at SCoR after I left California. We are still in contact with each other.]

Chapter Sixteen

Spirit is Bigger Than Perfectionism

Remember how I mentioned earlier that one had to be dressed appropriately for platform work? Infinite Intelligence is more than our man-made rules. You don't have to be "perfect" to be an instrument of Spirit. God's map is a bird's eye view compared to our limitations. Just be open to being useful.

The following blog was written on Monday, November 7, 2022.

When: Sunday, November 6, 2022

Dear Readers,

I woke up after plenty of sleep. Our clocks changed one hour back, heralding the darker days ahead. The night before was spent partying with the pirates and privateers of my pirate re-enactment group, The Port Royal Privateers, of which I've been a member since 2005. We have an annual November event called "Evening at The Drunken Mermaid Tavern." This year, a brewery in Torrance, CA, was the setting for the fictional Drunken Mermaid Tavern.

I brought my Celtic harp, Irish penny whistles, and concertina, and we partied like it was 1691... eating, drinking, and being a merry band of singing sea brigands.

But I don't drink, so I had no hangover and no need to sleep until noon.

Jim was not available to spend Sunday with me and I didn't just want to stay home in front of the TV.

Perhaps, I ought to go to church. I wasn't scheduled for that Sunday, but I could just go as a congregant, versus a worker, and slip in to the back row. Heck, I didn't even bother to dress up. Cargo shorts for church it is!

I arrived during the healing meditation when the lights were off and quietly found a seat near the middle-to-back of the room. It was a rather light Sunday – just 8 people including me.

When the lights went back on, "Steve" was both the chairperson and the one giving the sermon [Steve will sometimes lead the hymns by playing his guitar]. But, I noticed that a few of the congregants were turning their heads around and looking at me as if Santa had come down the chimney to a living room with people still up. We waved quickly to each other and the service continued.

When it was time for Messages from Spirit, Steve announced that he would be one of the mediums, but he also invited a second medium on the platform. "Karla or Russell," he asked, "Would either of you like to come up to the platform?"

I looked at "Karla" on the couch (yes, we have a couch in the sanctuary), and she didn't appear to want to move. I was wearing cargo shorts and at least a button/collar shirt, so I guess that's me. If it's meant to be, it's meant to be, no matter how I appeared, and technically, I was the only Certified Medium at this church. The others were either just non-certified volunteers, or students still working on the MPI course.

I let Steve go first. I needed to focus and tune-in. I looked around the room, and there he was:

He [the sitter] was bald, probably in his 40's, with a beard/mustache, black t-shirt, jeans. He looked like one of those rugged reality TV stars who was involved with anything involving lumberjacks, dangerous outdoor experiments, Alaska king crab fishing, trucking in snow, hunting, and sledgehammers. And, he was a total stranger seated in the very back row, his arm casually draped across the back of the empty seat next to him.

By now, you should know that I come from the school of "pick on the stranger in the very back row." Why? Because reading for a stranger is challenging and rewarding. Picking on the person in the back row makes them feel included and ties the room together.

The man confirmed everything that I said. I told him that normally, I would receive ancestors because they would stand behind someone's shoulder. But not for him.

The spirit stood next to his shoulder...the spirit was even sitting in the empty chair which he had his arm draped. The position next to the shoulder represented a peer, like a brother, cousin, friend, significant other.

It was a man. They had been very close.

I felt the bumpiness of driving possibly off-road. It felt like road trips, perhaps into the wild.

There was star-gazing.

Left-behind boots, like hiking boots or combat boots. People often throw away or discard the clothes of the dead, but not these. They represented a lifestyle and adventures together. He would still be walking with this gentleman, in his "spirit boots."

When I was done, I silently gave thanks to my Guides for urging me to come to church that day. This stranger was meant to get a message from me.

After Steve and I took turns with the rest of the congregants, I thought that we were finished, but there was one more person to receive a message. I was not aware because the podium was blocking my view from this one person. It was "Billy."

The message came first. I saw him dressed like a Viking on a horse with his sword in front, charging ahead. I could hear the Bugs Bunny/Elmer Fudd cartoon parody of Wagner's "Ride of the Valkyries" playing in the background. The spirit giving the message was probably his mother...a lady who stood behind Billy's right shoulder. She was sticking a match under the back of his shoe and lighting it. She had this impatient feeling of, "Why isn't he moving forward? Why is he procrastinating? He needs to charge ahead..."

Billy acknowledged the message. He understood it, but you could tell he didn't want to hear it. Sorry, Billy...I'm just the telephone.

After the service, a young man wearing a Covid mask whom Steve read for wanted to know when I was next conducting a mediumship class. I told him November 27th.

I then slipped out, eager to go home and eat lunch.

CHAPTER SEVENTEEN

Comparing Yourself to Others and Psychometry

In your travels, you'll meet people below your grade and above your grade. The lesson here is to get out of your ego and stop comparing yourself to others.

I also happen to believe that psychometry (the psychic ability of reading information from an object, usually by touching it) is a "gateway ability" to other psychic and mediumship practices!

Date: The below blog entry and the actual incident occurred in late February of 2019.

Dear Readers,

The text I received on Saturday morning read:

"The Church Board wants to know if you will give messages tomorrow. The speaker is Austyn Wells. She usually packs the house and her messages are too long. Mike will talk to her, until we have three [mediums] on the platform, that will make it go faster. Remember, we have Development Class right after."

What? They want me (and Mike) to share the Platform with Austyn Wells, the celebrity medium? How can I possibly do this?

I have only seen Ms. Wells one time while attending the church. She is the occasional speaker/medium at our church (and others), but she is pretty busy with her own practice. She does tours, book signings, is on the radio, and leads workshops/seminars. Besides being a Spiritualist Medium, Austyn is also a certified grief counselor. She has her own website, has published oracle cards, and just published a new book earlier this month. (Her website is www.austynwells.com, and her book is "Soul Conversations.") When I saw her at the church, I was not yet practicing on the platform. She is confident, gives messages with true emotion, and has quite the following. When Austyn Wells comes to town, the seats in the tiny church are completely filled.

As I started to feel nervous, I suddenly got a message from my spirit guides that went something like, "This is your EGO rearing its ugly head. Mediums are never supposed to compare themselves with other mediums. Every medium is different. Everyone develops at their own pace. Your job, Russell, is to simply receive messages and clearly communicate them to the living. It doesn't matter who happens to be standing next to you. You have a job to do, so do it well."

And then I calmed down.

Sunday was packed. It was a mix of church regulars, along with Austyn's fans. Austyn gave a very short sermon, which made sense, because everyone in the church needed to get a message. And, the Board had spoken to Austyn beforehand, explaining that she would need to cut down her time per person.

Unlike the British Spiritualist churches which allow a platform medium to spend a lot of time on a few people, but only a select few of the congregation get chosen, the Monrovia church was different in that they encouraged mediums to give every person in the room a message, if they want one. But, that means keeping it short and simple.

Because I had taken the focus off of me, I found that the psychic impressions flowed more smoothly and that I actually had "fun" being in the flow and delivering messages in between Austyn and Mike.

Austyn impressed my boyfriend, Jim, whom she never met. She pegged him as a writer who had lost a lot of friends when he was younger.

At some point, I felt directed to give a message to a particular woman in the very back. She was tall, elegant-looking, and well-dressed. But, when I stood up, she was gone. She had slipped away to use the restroom. I said out loud, "Oh, I wanted to give a message to the lady with the long brown hair in the very back, but I guess she stepped away."

Austyn said, "That is 'Brenda'. If you feel you have a message for her, Russell, you can give it to her when she gets back." I am guessing that Brenda is one of Austyn's fans. I had never seen her before, and when Austyn walked into the church, this lady immediately greeted Austyn with a hug.

"Well, in the meantime," I said, "I will approach Linda. Linda, would you like a message from Spirit?" Linda agreed. While I was giving Linda's message to her, Brenda returned and sat down. I immediately told Brenda that I was going to place her "on hold" as I continued with Linda's message.

I told Linda that her mother showed up in a wheelchair, banging her cane on the side of it. Of course, spirits don't need wheelchairs and canes, but it's a way for them to identify themselves. Linda's mom showed me an image of the two of them about to have a nice tea, with lovely bone china. As soon as the mom put the cup down, she took a deep breath and went into a "practical talk" with her daughter. I told Linda that I wasn't going to go over everything in front of everyone. I could tell her later in private. But one of those things had to do with a leak in the house, and to please get it fixed. Linda nodded in agreement.

After I "hung up" on Linda's mother, I turned my attention to Brenda in the back row.

I looked at Austyn and she nodded and smiled her approval for me to continue with Brenda.

"Hi, Brenda, I'm Russell. May I give you a message from Spirit, please?" Brenda stood up from her chair and said yes.

"Brenda, as I step into your vibration, I am seeing something from your past. I see an inflatable clown—a stand-up punching bag that will right itself after you've hit it. But, instead of the clown's face, I see your face superimposed on the punching bag. And I see these two males punching you back and forth. You wobble, but stand right up again.

"The face on the inflatable punching bag is a constant smile. This tells me that you didn't do anything...not because you were afraid to say anything, but that you didn't want to cause trouble or waves. You were looking for approval, and trying to please others. You felt that at that time, suffering builds character. So, you put up with being the punching bag.

"But, there are many other ways of building good character that don't involve having to suffer for it. The lady who is giving me this image – I don't know who she is, but she is holding your hand and wants to congratulate you at how far you've come, and how much you've grown. Does this make sense to you?"

Brenda was fighting back tears and she said, "Yes, Russell. 100 percent."

"And with that, I will leave you with Blessings from Spirit," I concluded.

Austyn then stood up since it was her turn to choose someone, but she looked at Brenda and added after me, "Remember, Brenda, Weebles Wobble, but they don't fall down!" For those too young to remember, Weebles were egg-shaped toys of people, maybe 2 inches tall. They were weighted on the bottom, so no matter what position you put them in, they would right themselves. The TV commercial at the time said, "Weebles wobble, but they don't fall down!" It was just confirmation that Brenda would be OK no matter how many "punches" she took in the past.

On the way home in the car, I asked Jim how he felt things went. Jim told me that while I was giving messages, Austyn was smiling at me with admiration. And, when I delivered Brenda her message, Austyn was nodding in total agreement. Since I normally keep my eyes closed, I didn't see any of this.

That evening, I emailed Austyn to thank her for visiting the church and to give her my mailing address so that she could ship me an autographed copy of her book (I paid her cash after church, but we were both too busy shortly thereafter). She emailed me back and said that she thought I did a good job on Platform.

Wow! Although it wasn't necessary, it was nice to receive kudos from a celebrity medium.

While Austyn was in the back of the church signing copies of her book, the rest of us were busy setting up for Development Class. Reverend Ernest Leard allowed me to conduct the meditation portion of the class.

Then, we did a psychometry exercise. We each put into a basket some kind of personal object, while not allowing the others at the table see what we were placing. Then, the basket was passed around and without looking, we reached into the basket and tried to pull out an object that didn't belong to us.

- I pulled out a silver ring.

- As I held the ring, I started scribbling information down on a pad of paper. I drew or wrote the following:

- Lighthouse on a cliff

- A raging fire at sea (an oil slick on fire, or a ship on fire)

- "Iona" and "Skye" (these are islands around Scotland)

- A Celtic cross

- The word "MARCH" (wasn't sure if this was the month of March, or the orders to "MARCH!)

- Some other things that I forgot.

When it came to my turn, I held up the ring. "To whom does it belong?" It was Ernie's ring. He said that the images I saw were of when he was in the Navy. The lighthouse seemed appropriate – one of Ernest's articles appeared in the National Spiritualist Magazine, and the front cover had a lighthouse on it. The raging fire at sea was a ship on fire. A friend of theirs survived but was badly burned. From that day forward, the sailor's nickname was "Crispy Critter." Ernest said his heritage was Irish, and that he visited Ireland. But, Iona and Skye are Scottish, I told him. Yes, they are...but he had to pass through them to get to Ireland back then. The Celtic cross seemed to fit. And "March" may have been related to Ernest's earlier years in the military.

I don't remember the words I wrote down, but Ernest asked me where they came from. I said that the words felt "male" like a male Guide or male spirit whom Ernest knew. Ernest nodded and seemed to have a nostalgic look when I mentioned the words. He requested that he have the sheets of paper because he wanted to show his family (they also studied mediumship).

CHAPTER EIGHTEEN

Psychometry with Blocks of Wood; Surprise the Medium!

Psychometry exercises can be done using participants' personal objects (keys, jewelry, watches, photos, etc.). But, what if you want to escape the temptation to profile and narrow down someone in the group by the object itself? That's easy...use identical pieces of wooden blocks assigned to each participant.

This entry is another example of spirits revealing artifacts belonging to the sitter. What I was not expecting was that all the artifacts described also happened to be sealed and hidden with the sitter at that very moment.

Dear Readers,

When: Sunday, December 8, 2019, at the Monrovia church

After working for the police department for over 19 years, I figured I'd never be surprised. I felt that I've seen/heard everything.

A Reverend, whom I'll call Julie Kinsale to protect her privacy, Mike and I were on the platform giving spirit greeting messages to the congregation. It was my turn, so I asked Reverent Ernest Leard in the very back row if he would like a message.

"Ernie" (as we casually refer to him) was once an officer in the US Navy, lived in Virginia, then moved to California with his family. At the time of this writing, he leads our development classes on the 2nd and 4th Sunday afternoons, after the church service.

I also chose to give a message to Ernie because he was in the back row. Try to pick on people in the back rows to tie the room together, and so they don't feel left out. It also helps with your speaking skills on projecting your voice.

"As we step into your vibration, I am seeing an older gentleman behind you. He feels like grandfather energy, but when I look at his surroundings, it looks Old World and much greener than California. He is wearing a pageboy hat that was common in the 1920 – 1930's, and is smoking a pipe.

"He is showing me a game in which an item is passed from one to another, or hidden, and you have to guess who has the object. I feel this is symbolic in that you may have lost something small and valuable. But, it's like a game...if you wait long enough, the item will finally come to you.

"He is also showing me something soft and delicate in your possession – it's like a pretty doily or lacey handkerchief. An heirloom. Don't throw it out. Even if it has a small stain, just cover it up with a vase or a small dish! Anyway, I hope that this makes sense to you, and I will leave you with blessings from Spirit."

Ernie spoke loudly enough so that I could hear him from the back row: "Yes, Russell, that made a lot of sense. Please make sure that we have time to talk this afternoon. I will need to fill out an affidavit for you."

I thanked him, but was still clueless. After church service, we got busy with moving chairs back, setting up folding tables, the donation basket (the money goes towards photocopying, notebooks, pens, etc.) brewing coffee, and getting snacks out since development class was held during the lunch hour. When we got seated, Ernie immediately turned to me and brought out three envelopes. I had a feeling I knew what these envelopes were for. It was in case some of us forgot to bring our blocks of wood to class for the psychometry exercise.

"Blocks of wood?"

Two weeks earlier, Ernie passed around a basket containing small, square blocks of wood. Each piece was numbered. We were to each take one block and look at the number, but don't let anyone else know the number we chose. Our assignment was to carry the block of wood and be in contact with it as much as possible until the next class. We could put it in our pockets, sleep with it under our pillows, keep it next to us at work, etc. The idea was for the block of wood to "soak up" our vibrations. Then, at class, we would toss the pieces back into the basket, number facing down, mix them up, then reach in and grab a block that does NOT have the number belonging to us. We would take turns describing the vibrations we were getting from the piece of wood. Then, we would show the number on the block, and the person it belonged to would then confirm or deny the information.

The reason Ernie brought the envelopes from home was because in case someone forgot their block of wood, they could "read" the contents of the sealed envelope so they weren't being left out of the exercise. If the proverbial "dog ate my homework," we had plenty of extra homework for you!

But, since we all remembered to bring our blocks of wood, there was no need to read the three envelopes.

But, apparently, with the help of Spirit, I did exactly that during the message portion of church less than an hour earlier.

Ernie opened the envelopes one at a time and showed the contents to me, and to the rest of the class.

"This was my father, Russell." OK, so I got father/grandfather mixed up, because Ernie is older than most baby-boomers, but it made sense because the clothes in the black and white photo matched my description, which was 1920-1930...and the man was proudly displaying his pipe.

Ernie opened the second envelope and produced old, dented military dog-tags. It belonged to his father. Ernie had lost them and could not locate them. Instead of driving himself crazy trying to find them, he decided to "give up" and trust that they would eventually be discovered – which they were!

Ernie opened the third envelope. He pulled out a delicate piece of fabric with embroidered floral designs on the edge of the cloth. It was once white, but had faded to an off-white. It was a handkerchief owned by his father, probably given to him by his mother.

Now, it's one thing to receive verbal confirmation a few weeks later. But, for the sitter to happen to have those actual items on-hand on that very morning they were described by spirit to the medium, then from the medium to the sitter?

"But wait…there's MORE!"

Not counting Ernie, there were seven of us attending development class that Sunday. I would have to say that everyone did a fine job. I was especially pleased to see the students who often say, "I can't get anything…I never get anything" actually received accurate information.

Robin clutched her piece of wood and announced to the group that the person who carried this block of wood for the past 2 weeks was, at the age of 17, seeking spiritual answers. This person was not satisfied with the mainstream religion's teachings, and he wanted to find his own path and seek his own answers. His search began as a teenager, around 17. Robin looked straight at me and said, "For some reason, and I don't know why, I kept getting an image of Russell." She then revealed the number "17" on the piece of wood.

Number 17 was my block of wood. And, everything she mentioned was true. This was not a case of "process of elimination" because Robin was the very first person to volunteer.

Also, to eliminate the crossing of "process of elimination" with "adding on information as an afterthought once we know who the person is," we each scribbled on our notepads the information we received while we held the blocks of wood, before any of us could speak our findings. That way, we could not conveniently "change" the information verbally, once it was written on paper.

I don't remember what Jim told "Irma"…they were the last two left, so we knew that Jim and Irma had each other's blocks of wood. But I saw what

Jim wrote on his notepad before we all started talking. It turns out that he was describing a lady's features – and those features were those of Irma!

In short, it was a great Sunday!

I really like this psychometry exercise in which you substitute identical pieces of wood with numbers on them for personal items like keys and jewelry.
If I were holding someone's keychain shaped like a shamrock, it would be easy for me to profile that person as either having Irish heritage, connections to Ireland, or liking Irish music and culture. And I could still be wrong, if the owner was simply given the keychain from someone who happened to have visited Ireland and just needed any keychain. No...identical pieces of wood are more impersonal and "force" the medium to not make assumptions.
It can be very inexpensive to do this exercise. Obtain from an arts and crafts store a package of wooden tiles or even popsicle sticks. Using permanent ink, number each one. You can always go over the number and create more if you think you already know how many are participating. Have each person choose a piece of wood, while not revealing to the group which number they picked. They will keep this piece of wood with them until you all meet up again. Throw all the wooden pieces into a bag or hat and have everyone pick one, making sure it was not theirs. Write down your psychometric impressions on paper.
As the organizer, it is a good idea to mention multiple times to the participants to remember to bring with them their piece of wood to

the development circle, even reminding them to check to make sure it's on them before leaving their homes.

Doing a Reading Over the Phone

I think my one piece of advice when doing mediumship over the phone is to use a headset. You could put the phone down and put it on speaker mode, but this can distort sound. If you thought my advice would be the difference in the dynamics between phone versus in-person, nope! To me, it's exactly the same, but sometimes easier because your "blindness" actually gives you more freedom. The following entry was one of my first attempts at mediumship over the phone.

When: Friday, September 15, 2017 at 8:00 p.m.

Where: I was seated in front of my spirit/ancestor altar in the living room.

Sitter: Michelle (newspaper journalist, San Gabriel Valley), pet-sitting at a friend's home.

Dear Readers,

I treat my sessions as confidential. If I use anecdotes and illustrations, no names are mentioned. However, Michelle has agreed that I can share this information with her friend who works in my building. Our mutual friend works in Fiscal Operations Division, LAPD.

Confirmation Notes were covered after the session was "closed down." However, for the sake of continuity, I have included any confirmations along with the spirit communications in these notes.

This was an experiment at mediumship over the phone. I did not meet Michelle in person, nor did I speak with her before the session. I was introduced through email by a mutual friend/co-worker in the Police Headquarters Facility. Because the subconscious mind protects the Ego, the only memories I have of the session were "confirmation-hits." Everyone likes approval and validation! I have very little memories of the "misses" and the information not confirmed. Hopefully, Michelle can remember to fill in any blanks of information that I was not accurate with, or unconfirmed information that might possibly be confirmed at a later date, either through sudden memories, or a 3rd party (if Michelle prefers to pursue that information).

At the appointed time, I called Michelle and kept the "hello's" brief, and went into trance. First thing I saw was on mother's side of family, a sepia picture of a woman from the Edwardian Era. Not sure what this was and did not mention anything to Michelle. I asked her if she knew about her family going back to the late 1800's into the early 1900's, and Michelle replied she was only familiar with current family. I asked Spirit for confirmation and evidence applying to current time and dismissed the Edwardian Era woman.

Uncle energy appearing on mother's side of the family. Pat Boone hair, meaning it's straight and kept neat. Small mark on the face, like Madonna's mole. Nice smile. Dressed up in red, and red/white. Saw him with Michelle as a little girl, next to a big horse. Michelle is wearing a child's cowboy hat (with red edge/trim).

Michelle believes this to be an uncle who worked for Disneyland as a musician. He would dress up in a red suit coat, sometimes red and white stripes. Picture barbershop quartet/Dick Van Dyke from Mary Poppins styles of clothes, but with red and white. He sometimes played music with the band, while being pulled by Clydesdale horses. He brought her to Disneyland to see the horses. Michelle confirms that she was a tomboy growing up and would dress like a cowboy, with a pellet gun, little cowboy boots, and leave the house that way. Spirit showed me a unique picture frame connected to Uncle and Michelle. She confirmed that her mother still has it. The picture is a young Michelle riding on Uncle's shoulders. I then saw him blowing through an instrument, then handing it to young Michelle. She said that the wind instruments were difficult for her to learn, but her uncle could play the clarinet, then tried to have her play it. She still has trouble with the wind instruments.

A man appeared on father's side of family. He is stern-looking. Eyebrows are arched in disapproval. Scowl. Gray hair. Neatly dressed. He had a "George Hamil-tan" meaning he had a darker complexion compared to other family members, reminiscent of actor George Hamilton who had a perpetual tan. Booze bottle in one hand. I did not mention the booze bottle because I was embarrassed about saying he was a drunkard, but I did tell Michelle that this man had "substance abuse problems." She said this man is her father.

I saw him building up inside to the breaking point, them blowing up at everyone in a temper. He is giving his wife small, blue flowers in bunches of 3 and 4. 3 symbolizes communications. 4 symbolizes stability. To me, he is apologizing to his wife (who is still alive) that he was not a good communicator in life (he yelled, couldn't control his feelings), and apologized for not being stable. My logic kicked in briefly (which is not proper for keeping a connection). This father looked proper and well-put-together. He was a control freak. How could he apologize for an unstable household?

Michelle said that he himself was unstable. They never knew what mood he'd be in. Ahhh…makes sense. Michelle also mentioned that the small, blue flowers were placed on his coffin or grave by her mother. The father is apologizing to Michelle for being very hard on her and feeling as if whatever she accomplished was never good enough. He was holding out an apple. The apple, to me, is my symbol for higher learning and education. School work. Although he was not stable, he valued education. Michelle confirmed this by telling me that her father prematurely removed her from high school and put her in college.

Editing on my part: I made the error of not spitting out the truth. I saw a booze bottle in her father's hand, yet I held back and simply said "substance abuse problem." It wasn't until after the session when we did Confirmation Notes that she revealed her father was an abusive man who was an alcoholic. This practice is not about me and my ego of being scared that I might be wrong. If I am the vessel, I need to remove myself and let the message flow.

A woman appeared on father's side, but is not a blood relative. She knew Michelle's father and family. She gives off an aunt-like energy. Quiet and kind. Doesn't always reveal all her feelings. She is overweight and buxom. She wears autumn and earth colors, like dark yellows, tans, browns. She is in the kitchen, and enjoys doing crafts with her fingers that require threads or yarn. She loves to dance and is showing Michelle how to dance.

However, because of her weight issue, she cannot move her feet around too much, so she shows her expressions through the movements of her arms, hands and fingers. Michelle confirmed this woman to be a neighbor whom she often visited when she was a little girl. She cooked and did sewing. She was Greek/Greek origins. She danced expressively using her arms, hands, fingers, upper body, but not so much her legs/feet. She wore autumn colors. She was on the quiet side.

Death Confirmations: I am still trying to work with Spirit on the causes of death or circumstances surrounding the deaths. I forgot which disease belonged to which spirit (the uncle and the Greek neighbor), but in one I felt my fingertips tingle which indicates diabetes/diabetic complications. In the other, I felt it was coronary-related/cholesterol/arterial.

For the father, I specifically received a tingling then numbing sensation going up both legs, both arms, then slowly my torso. I didn't know how to interpret this except that it was like nerve damage or a nerve problem occurring. Michelle said he died from brain cancer. The brain is connected to the central nervous system, so in a way this makes sense. But I think a clairvoyant image of the brain might be better.

I'm a little scared of receiving a clairsentient headache, so I am wondering if this fear prevented me from feeling that he died of a brain complication? However, I didn't mind receiving clairsentient abdominal pains when one spirit indicated he was shot 3 times in his abdomen, or when an Australian spirit (the father of my Australian-American friend) indicated that the doctors and nurses had to continually remove fluids from his abdomen right before he died.

In conclusion to Death Confirmations, I think that clairsentience can only go so far. I would like to receive more information through clairvoyance, clairaudience, or even better—claircognizance, which would just be awesome. Back to Michelle's session...

The session went for about 30 minutes, which is the prescribed time for a private sitting, according to one medium author's advice. So, the next 10 minutes were devoted to questions and answers. When this was finished, I started to close up the session when her Disneyland-employed uncle suddenly came back. He wanted to put in his last two cents...what a character!

I told Michelle that your uncle is giving you a rose and JANIS JOPLIN. Not the spirit of Janis Joplin, but something square, like maybe a record album cover? Or a poster of her? Then I closed the session. Michelle revealed to me that she was in the middle of reading a book – a biography of Janis Joplin.

Michelle wanted to give me constructive criticism. After all, this is an experiment at phone reading and I welcomed anything. She said that I need to be more confident in myself and not hold back. I can speak up and say things. Most of what I communicated was spot-on and I need to trust myself more. Although I was not asking for payment, she said that she'd like to keep in touch, and perhaps the three of us could go out for lunch or dinner. She definitely wants to treat me to a meal.

The session itself, not counting Confirmation Notes, was approximately 40 minutes.

On the Subject of Altars

In the previous chapter when I did a phone reading, I sat down at an altar. The religion/philosophy/science of modern Spiritualism does not require anything like an altar or shrine with various paraphernalia arranged around, below, and on top of it. The medium is the sacred tool — not the items she collects or the magical jewelry he wears. Spirits will show up wherever they need to show up, not in front of any altar.

That being said, many mediumship-development teachers often mention that doing one's practice and meditation in the same room, at the same time, and sometimes even in the same chair, is beneficial for development. They often say that it's also good for the spirits when the medium establishes a regular practice in the same place every time. The regularity is supposed to build up energy within a specific space, like a mini-version of the various sacred power centers on the planet that people take pilgrimages to experience.

In our modern world, it's not always practical to meditate in the same place and same time, but I can understand the method behind the training. As an anthropology graduate, I like to compare and contrast different cultures, and I have noticed that with other religions that do employ material culture, that this meeting place in between humans and the spirit world is an altar or shrine. A personal altar or shrine is a great place to meditate, hold a séance, do divination, and give one's gratitude to the spirits.

Again, it's not needed in Spiritualism, but as humans with culture, I think it's natural for us to want to visibly establish a sacred space with items of a symbolic nature. Even I, the minimalist, keep an altar with pictures of my dead relatives, candles, incense, and items that represent my spirit guides.

I have seen altars on top of card tables, book shelves, on the floor, on a wall shelf, even inside a closet space.

I feel it's a very personal thing if you choose to set up an altar. You can have items on it that speak to you in a spiritual way, and have items that the spirits themselves might ask you to place there. Some tips and suggestions:

- Fire safety. Jar candles and tea lights surrounded by glass are probably safer than exposed tapers. I have seen smaller jar candles and tea lights in glass votive holders placed in large glass bowls filled with water. I still recommend that if you are leaving the dwelling that all flames be respectfully extinguished, including burning incense.

- If you want it to be inconspicuous, the surface can have a white doily or handkerchief, a votive candle, a few pictures of your ancestors, and a vase of flowers. "Move on...there's nothing paranormal happening here, folks..."

- Feeling creative? If you happen to know how your spirit guides manifest themselves to you, perhaps a representation on the altar is a nice touch. For example, one of my guides manifests himself as an old Chinese master or wise man, so I have a ceramic figurine of a smiling, bald Buddha-like character that I picked up in a Chinatown on my travels. Another guide manifests as a Viking warrior, so he is represented with a Viking figurine I brought back from Reykjavic, Iceland.

CHAPTER TWENTY

Short Examples of Clairsentience

If clairvoyance is "clear seeing," then clairsentience is "clear feeling." If you pick up an emotional state surrounding someone without being in their presence, you would be experiencing a form of clairsentience. The spirit can also impress physical sensations on the medium's body to convey information. If you want Spirit to use this method but are scared of the feelings being too intense, you can tell Spirit to be subtle with the feelings that it sends.

The following examples which never made journal entries are real examples of clairsentience:

- A P-III named "Marissa" who worked just around the corner from Office of Operations on the 3rd Floor for CSOC (Community Safety Operations Center) became friends with me. One day, I felt Marissa's father come through to visit her. With her permission, I described his clothing style accurately, his coin collection, and his need to apologize to his daughter for the horrible things he said when she was younger. Marissa was crying tears of relief because she needed to hear this from her father (she never spoke to me about her relationship with her parents). But, when I asked how he died, I kept getting shivers starting in my fingertips and running up the length of my arms to my body. "What does that mean?" I asked myself. No answer. So, I described the sensation to Marissa. She said, "My father died from being accidentally electrocuted while he was working on some wires without protective gloves."

- While working in Office of Operations, I sat across from a detective who had an open mind about paranormal phenomenon. She told me that her deceased father was one of the reasons she wanted to become a detective. When I silently asked how he died, I immediately felt three sharp sensations occurring in my lower left abdomen. I told her what I was feeling and didn't understand what it meant. She told me that when her father was sitting in his vehicle, a suspect went up to his rolled-down window and shot him 3 times in the abdomen. While the suspect was never caught, the incident encouraged his daughter to pursue the path of being a detective.

- On a more humorous note, while on the platform at church, I was connecting a spirit to a sitter when I suddenly felt myself grow boobs, gain 100 pounds, fluttering my arms and hands and bouncing on my feet. I described the spirit as an overweight woman who was very extroverted and loved to run and bounce around. The sitter said that she knew exactly who this deceased friend of hers was. I concluded saying, "She was very much the social butterfly—although a very heavy butterfly!"

Creating Clairsentient Codes—say that 3 times fast! You can make up agreements with your spirit guides for clairsentient codes. For example, a tightness in your chest could mean cardiac issues or lung issues. Tingling fingertips could mean diabetes. A headache could mean head trauma or brain issues. There is no right or wrong, because it would be your own personal list.

CHAPTER TWENTY-ONE

Is It Mediumship or ESP?

Extrasensory Perception is perceiving information from the sitter without using the 5 senses. Some psychics say that the reader is receiving the information from the memories of the sitter. Mediumship, however, is supposed to be information being given directly to the medium, independent of the sitter.

The following example is how both the medium and the sitter felt that it was indeed mediumship. Although information might not be confirmed immediately, I encourage student mediums to aim for third-party confirmations.

Since this example never made it into "True Tales From the Platform," I don't have a specific date.

"Jake" and I met on the same train taking us to downtown Los Angeles. We both worked for the City, but in different departments.

One early morning, we had one of the train cars to ourselves. From an earlier discussion on the topic of mediumship, I felt that Jake's father was visiting us on the train. I asked Jake's permission if I could bring his father forward.

I was accurate in describing Jake's Australian father to him, including the physical situation in the hospital before he passed. However, there was one bit of information that did not resonate with Jake. I had a clairsentient feeling of half my face slumping or losing all its muscle tone. I asked Jake if he remembered his father suffering from a stroke or Bell's palsy causing half his face to slump?

Jake had no recollection of this. I chalked it up to an error on my part and let it go.

The next morning on the train, Jake told me that when he got home yesterday, he phoned his sister back in Australia and asked her if their father had any symptoms like this? His sister said that after Jake had gotten married and moved to the USA, that their father indeed suffered from something that caused half his face to lose muscle control temporarily.

Since I don't know Jake's family members back in Australia, and since Jake had no memory of this happening to his father, my conclusion is that his father in spirit was giving me this news.

Does Psychic Information Feel Different From Mediumship Information?

All mediums are psychics, but not all psychics are mediums. Can you feel the difference between whether the information you are picking up is psychic information from the sitter, versus mediumship information?

This is not easy to describe because all mediums and psychics are different. When I first started out with mediumship, it was difficult to tell the difference. Now, I was used to receiving psychic information before 2017. Perhaps it's best to describe the feeling between psychic information and one's imagination.

For me, psychic information feels different from imagination in that it appears and doesn't seem to fade away immediately. When I question the information, it does not appear to change or disappear. Also, imagination seems more "forced"—like I desperately want some news to appear, versus nothing at all appearing (which can be terrifying), so I wish hard for anything—and my imagination will take over just to fill the gap in my mind. Psychic information will appear when it appears, and when I feel relaxed and centered. I cannot force it to occur. When it does come through, it appears to me like I am remembering a commercial I saw on TV.

How can I tell the difference between psychic information and mediumship information? Psychic information feels like it comes easier to me because it's about the person in front of me. That seems to be an easy connection. Mediumship information is coming from a spirit separate from the sitter and me, so it has a more "above and beyond" feeling, and a little "finer" and more subtle. Also, if it's coming from a spirit, I can sometimes feel the attitude of the spirit behind the information. Maybe the spirit was sarcastic or had dark humor when alive. The information coming through will have that feeling backing it up. Psychic information being picked up from the sitter will have a more detached feeling, even if the content of the information is very emotional.

Also, with psychic information, it's mostly about the sitter and what they are going through. Mediumship information is usually about the spirit in question, although the spirit can share information to the medium about the sitter—if this is the case, it feels like the information is coming from an outside source, versus from the sitter to me.

Chapter Twenty-Two

On the Subject of Dark Entities

There seem to be two schools of thought on the subject of preventing dark entities, trickster spirits, and nasty unwanted things dropping in. I've discovered these two viewpoints based on my own experience and from talking to others.

These two thoughts aren't necessarily opposed to each other. A medium can fall somewhere in the middle, and truth is sometimes not always black and white.

The first is that one should always do a spiritual cleansing and prayers of protection before beginning any reading, I believe in the power of prayer and proper intention, so this makes sense. Spiritual cleansing can be done through visualization and meditation, and/or using external tools and ingredients (white candles, burning sage, sprinkling Florida Water or holy water, etc.) The medium would also pray for the light of protection and safety, along with any spirit guides and angels to guard the medium.

The second is that the medium's personal life, sense of morals and ethics (or the lack thereof) is a magnet for matching energies. We call this the

Law of Attraction. So, while a medium might be a law-abiding citizen on the outside with a zero crime record, if he carries an invisible chip on his shoulder all the time, likes to engage in harmful gossip, has a vindictive and vengeful personality, mistrusts others, has a cynical world view, loves playing the victim or the martyr, and loves to engage in arguments, imagine this kind of aura attracting similar spirits. I also believe in this method of protection through clean living, and that by doing psychological and spiritual inner work to clear up one's hang-ups, issues, and inner demons, then life runs more smoothly and you attract to yourself the positive. Your own energy is what protects you and attracts good things and serendipitous events into your life — not an ingredient or an object from a metaphysical store.

If you are working with a group (church, séance, development circle, gallery demonstration), I would suggest doing the spiritual cleansing and prayers of protection because you don't know what kind of psychic magnets your fellow participants are and what they've dragged in.

Again, both can be used effectively. If I had a choice, I would choose the second opinion because it involves true inner healing, which in turn, affects one's outer environment. While the purpose of learning mediumship is to prove the existence of life after death through spirit communication, the NSAC states that the main purpose of mediumship is the unfoldment of the individual.[1]

Prevention is better than a cure.

---

1. NSAC Spiritualist Manual, Twentieth Edition. National Spiritualist Association of Churches, Lily Dale, New York, 2017.

Sitting in the Power, My Version

There are many ways to sit in one's power. While it is sometimes called a "meditation," it is more like an active preparation for mediumship. It not only raises your vibration to get closer to the more subtle spirit energies, it also helps the spirits when they try to connect to the medium. It's like two landline phones. In order for them to work, there must be wiring and telephone poles connecting the two phones. Sitting in the power is like creating and building the telephone wires between the two phones.

I have experimented with different versions. Some of them are rather complicated. This is the current method that I use when preparing for any form of mediumship — whether private or public, in-person or online.

While seated or standing, I visualize being grounded to the planet.

I leave through the top of my head and travel quickly above my city, the planet, past the solar system...

I travel towards a white light of amazing brilliance and merge with that light. I greet the spirit world and send it my love. I imagine that I am receiving love from the spirit world in return.

Then, I am ready to begin.

When I am finished, I give thanks to the spirit world and I go backwards with the steps, descending through space, back to Earth, above my city, above the building, and gently descend into my seated (or standing) body, grounding once more. I also imagine drawing up the energy of the earth up into my feet, then up the rest of my body, stopping at the top of my head.

That's it.

CHAPTER TWENTY-THREE

We Covered Trains and Automobiles...What About Airplanes?

I've always felt that one of the differences between a ghost and a spirit is that a ghost is often limited to a specific locale (cemetery, building, location of death or favorite place when alive). Ghosts appear to ignore you and repeat actions and movements, while spirits appear intelligent, can interact, and can drop in anywhere at any time.

The following blog entry illustrates that spirits can drop in at any time, even inside an Airbus A350.

Dear Readers,

"Ladies and Gentlemen, please fasten your seatbelts, your tray tables stowed and locked, and your seats in the upright position. We will be landing soon at Singapore Changi Airport," said the captain over the public announcement system.

Using the electronic buttons near my armrest, I operated my business class seat to the neutral landing/takeoff position. I gazed out the window at the early sunrise over the Indonesian and Malaysian islands that surrounded the tiny island-nation of the Republic of Singapore (aka, the "Crazy Rich Asians" country). While I am a native Californian, my parents were from Singapore.

Eariler, in September of 2019...

My mother and I were traveling on an inaugural 15-hour flight from Seattle to Singapore. We had never experienced an inaugural flight on a new Airbus A350-900 Ultra-Long Range, so there was cake, champagne, hors d'oeuvres, balloons, Chinese lion dancers, speeches, promotional gift bags, and a ribbon-cutting ceremony at the gate in Seattle. I saw pictures of the business class seats. They were these somewhat isolated "pods" which allowed the passenger some privacy, and the seats could be turned into flat beds.

Sometime during the night portion of the flight, I was chatting with one of the flight attendants. The pod I was seated in allowed me to have a conversation without feeling that I was disturbing the other sleeping passengers around me. Since the country of Singapore is a mix of different cultures and languages, this particular flight attendant was originally from India. We were talking about spiritual topics, and the similarities and differences between the East and the West on mysticism. I was discussing the chakras (energy wheels that help control the human aura), when I slipped into "psychic mode" and ended up giving her a psychic/non-mediumistic reading based upon her aura, and her past-present-future.

On Final Approach...

It was early morning when I opened my window shade. The Indian flight attendant must have been impressed, because as we were coming in for landing, she came back to my seat with one of her female colleagues from a different section of the airplane (Premium Economy Class). Since the class sections are hidden from view during the flight, I had not seen this second flight attendant during our entire flight.

At first, I thought they were going to see my mother in the business class seat in front of mine. My mother sometimes will adjust the necks/spines of flight attendants on long flights as a favor to them. But no...they were here to see me. She apologized terribly for the interruption and for putting me on the spot.

"Mr. Chan, this is Ms. ____________. I was hoping that maybe you could help her, since you explained that you are a student medium. She just lost her father and is handling it with difficulty. I'm so sorry for putting you on the spot..."

I looked at the new flight attendant. She hid her sorrow well, like a good flight attendant, and stood there smiling her "welcome aboard" smile.

I didn't like to be put on the spot, especially when we are about to land. I didn't want to fail and look stupid in front of the flight attendant. But, I do have a soft spot for them, like I do for cops. I understand flight attendant culture. Everything is "at-the-moment, on-the-spot." It's a stressful, hectic, exciting life, punctuated with brief connections. The Indian flight attendant left us alone to talk. I explained to the new flight attendant that I could not promise anything. After all, we are in an airplane, about to land, and I don't conjure up spirits on demand.

As I sat there trying to make up excuses to protect my ego, my guides kinda' pushed me and I slipped off the cliff. I knew it because I saw her father. I described him wearing a straw hat, his thin build yet sporting a beer belly, how he was actually shorter than her, the jokes he made with his wife about him and his mistresses (and her jokes back to him about her "boyfriends") , internal organ failure (liver), and his message to her that she was not finished – to keep studying and not to settle for a stewardess job. She was extremely grateful and immediately ran back to her jump seat, as fast as her native-inspired sarong uniform would allow.

As we glided to the runway on final approach, I gave thanks to my spirit guides that I didn't look like an idiot in front of the lovely crew.

CHAPTER TWENTY-FOUR

And Let's Not Forget Ships.

I f spirits can appear on planes, trains and automobiles, of course they can appear on cruise ships. Below is a reading that I shall never forget.

When: September 16, 2022, One week round-trip cruise to Alaska from Seattle.

Ahoy, Readers!

We were sailing from the Alaskan city of Skagway to Victoria, British Columbia, Canada. It was a full day at sea, so that meant that dinner was a "dress-to-impress" affair, should passengers wish to dine in the formal dining rooms, versus the all-you-can-eat buffet which has no dress code.

I came downstairs to the center of the ship which is a large, open space, multi-stories with beautiful stairs, glass elevators, plenty of lounges, bars, bistros, and a place for live entertainment. Since the main dining rooms are accessible from this space, I agreed to wait for my mother here before we entered the restaurant.

I must have been a memorable passenger, thanks to my funny homemade hats and unusual cruise attire, because one woman came up to me and told me that she and her husband had been watching me the whole cruise. They were from Texas, and she wanted to know more about my Victorian/Edwardian-looking formal attire and noticed that I had The Magician Tarot card stuck in my hat band.

I explained to her that I was dressed "steampunk" which is a look based upon the fantasy style of what Victorian and Edwardian people might have envisioned the world of science fiction. I also told her that I worked for the police department back home and that I played the Celtic harp.

She looked very surprised and said that she never met anyone quite like me. I never think about it, but I guess that would be a true statement. I know people who knit and crochet. I know people who play the harp. I know Tarot card readers. I know people who have done stage acting, have flown airplanes, have been to all the Seven Continents, have published poetry, and have taught classes in basic psychic development. But, I don't know that many individuals who have done all of the above.

I explained to her the meaning behind The Magician Tarot card. To me, it meant someone who mastered his environment and was in balance of the physical, philosophical, emotional, and mental worlds. I revealed to her that I owned over 30 Tarot card decks because I love the Tarot. While I explained this, I noticed she had a round sticker on her shirt of a young man, maybe in his late 20's to early 30's, possibly in memory of a loved one.

She asked me if the Tarot cards could assist in determining if the spirit of someone who passed was still around? I explained to her that the Tarot was a tool normally used in psychic readings for the querent: her love life, her career, her environment, her friends, family and enemies. But for the spirits of the dead? The cards themselves don't talk about the dead...she would need to contact a medium.

She had a desperate look in her eye, and I suddenly felt like I was "on the spot." She explained that she had lost her son (the picture on the sticker) just a few months ago and she thought of him constantly. She felt she could escape the pain by taking a cruise with her husband and another couple, but she couldn't get the pain of his death out of her mind.

I felt bad for her and I was on vacation, so I knew that I shouldn't interfere....but it was too late.

He showed up.

In fact, he appeared just beyond her right shoulder.

I told her (she introduced herself as "Dee") that I felt his presence very close to her. She was surprised and just looked at me with new eyes. I guess that was a shock considering all the other things I told her about myself.

"Normally, when a child in spirit shows up, he stands in front of the parent. But, you and I are talking very close to one another so there's no room, but I feel that the reason he is standing behind your right shoulder is because your son was much closer to your mother than he was to his grandmother on dad's side. Am I right?"

"Yes, absolutely...he was much more familiar with my parents!"

"Dee, I don't know how long he's going to be here, but I just want you to answer with a Yes, No, or I Don't Know if I should ask you for confirmation. Please do not confirm with any further information unless I specifically ask for it."

During this spontaneous sitting, I gathered the following, while Dee began to cry:

He was a people-pleaser. He focused much more on his personality because he secretly felt inadequate and wanted attention and approval. He gained approval from his mother and grandmother, but felt he had to earn it from other family and friends. Sadly, this was true.

I saw sports jerseys and sports t-shirts. He liked to play sports but was not very good at it. He probably got chosen last on school teams. He left behind a lot of sports jerseys and memorabilia. He enjoyed playing baseball but his mother said he wasn't very good.

He was stomping around furiously and repeating, "I'm sorry...I am so sorry...it was my fault!" He was blaming himself for the way he died, and apologized constantly to his mother that it was all his fault. What was all that about? Dee cried some more and said that he died of fentanyl overdose.

I saw a girl about his age. He told his mother to please don't blame this girl for whatever. It's not her fault. I don't know what that meant, but Dee understood and spoke the name of this girl. I told Dee that the girl didn't feel like a girlfriend or romantic interest, but that they were close. When they were together, they could potentially cause trouble together. Dee confirmed this.

I saw The Three Stooges. I felt that the son's humor was very juvenile, very physical, and very low-brow. I even saw male body parts and the jokes surrounding this. Dee laughed through her tears and said that I understood her son perfectly.

I also told her that his "karma" on the Other Side was to assist other souls crossing over who suffered the same things like drug overdose or suicide. So, I felt like he was putting himself to good use, but that it was not like "doing time" in prison...it was his spiritual community service to others who experienced the same thing. This really clicked with Dee because he had that kind of helping-hand attitude.

Dee asked me to tell him that she still loved him. I told her with a smile that he can already hear you, and that you don't need me – some perfect stranger – to tell him that! Besides, he was standing right next to her. Dee told me that I had given her great hope and that she wanted to hug me. She was feeling awful during the trip, but now things changed. She wanted to pay me in some way, but her wallet was locked inside the safe in her cabin.

I told her that there was one way that she could pay me.

I told her that if she ever found herself in the position of defending the concept of psychics and mediums, that she please defend our talents. I told her that yes, she or her loved ones might run into people who claim to be psychics and mediums, but who are frauds and fakes...heck, there are frauds and fakes in every religion and in every career. But, that the real and honest ones are out there, not trying to make a fast buck off of someone's vulnerability. If they did charge money, it would be just like how a counselor or therapist might charge for their time. I told her that I didn't need her money and that I was just some passenger who answered the call of Spirit to be of assistance, and that I had no need to take advantage of her vulnerable state. She absolutely agreed.

When we were coming to a close, her husband walked up to her. She gushed to him what I had done and he smiled politely but probably was very suspicious of the claims she made about me. Behind his polite southern smile, he probably thought, Who is this weirdo who caused my wife to shed tears in public?

I didn't care what he thought. I wasn't asking for money and I did what my spirit guides wanted me to do – be open to Spirit's call and to be a healer. Clearly, Dee needed healing closure. You know that saying, "I want to be the person my dog thinks I am"? Well, I substitute "dog" for "spirit guides."

The next evening, we were docked in Victoria, BC, Canada. Mom and I descended from our cabin on Deck 15 to Deck 14 because we heard that the ship's chapel had a condolence book in honor of Queen Elizabeth II's passing. My mother had been a British subject until 1965, when Singapore gained its independence from the Commonwealth. Then, she became Singaporean, and then a U.S. citizen in the early 1980's. But, she had very fond memories of singing "God Save The Queen" as a school girl under the British flag and she wanted to write something heart-felt in the chapel's book. While we made our way through the narrow hall of Deck 14, a door opened and out came Dee, her husband, and their friends.

Dee looked totally different. She looked happy and radiant. Her husband smiled a more genuine smile at me, probably because I looked like a normal, American passenger walking behind his elderly mother, and his wife's money was untouched.

Dee told me thank you, again, and asked if this was my mother. My mother must have looked confused because I didn't tell her about my mediumship session with Dee. She told my mother that I was very special and that she must be very proud of her son.

Positive, yet awkward.

I was just happy that Dee was happy.

"Our Naughty Grannies Can't Wait to Talk With You..."

This chapter has quite a few lessons. First, never profile a spirit. For example, just because an Asian spirit appears before you, don't assume that rice was their favorite food, or that the spirit was excellent in math and science.

Second, just because someone dies doesn't suddenly make them a saint. Yes, after death, the spirit gains a broadened perspective and an understanding of how their words and actions affected others while they were alive. Yes, they even come back to apologize for their wrongdoings. But, if they are trying to gain recognition from the sitter, they will display only those aspects to the medium that the sitter will recognize.

Third, while Spiritualist mediums working a NSAC function consider mediumship as a sacred task, the spirits that come through might not act very church-like. It is a careful balance for the platform medium to bring forth the true personality of the salty spirit, while still attempting to maintain platform decorum without resorting to cussing or lewd displays. The mediums also need to be able to re-word certain facts or use harmless euphemisms. I have personally found that the audience or congregation is much more forgiving if the medium accidentally gets a little ribald because they are being very honest in their description of the raunchy spirit. Sometimes, if the spirit has things to say that aren't appropriate in church, the medium is allowed to ask the sitter if they could meet up after the church service in the parking lot, or some private place.

A moment of nostalgia swept over me when I looked at the date of this entry (April of 2023). My living room was almost bare except for my spirit altar. Most items were already in my new home, my California condo was getting ready to be listed on the market, and retirement was within 2 months...

Dear Readers,

I didn't really want to do the phone reading.

It was a Tuesday after work, and Tuesdays were my time to just be lazy and eat dinner in front of the TV.

When I got home from LAPD, the store in which I do readings for (via phone or FaceTime) asked if I were available to give a mediumship reading for 60 minutes, if possible that evening. I knew that if I waited for another day, it would be very difficult, so I texted the scheduling office that I would be available for a 30-minute session only, starting at 7:00 p.m. I don't see why a private one-person mediumship session should take one hour. The store texted back the phone number of the client and said that 7:00 was fine.

I curled up on my couch to get a cat nap. I immediately felt "feminine" energy surrounding me regarding "Sheena" my 7:00 p.m. client. OK, I thought...no male relatives for tonight's session.

At 6:50 p.m., I sat at my altar, inserted my Bluetooth ear phones, and called Sheena. I explained to her what to expect, when and when not to ask questions, how to reply to me if I had a question for her (just YES, NO, or I DON'T UNDERSTAND), and that the store had a policy that if within the first 5 minutes she did not feel that I was "clicking" with her, she could terminate the session and get all her money back.

The first five minutes were rough! Yes, she wanted to contact someone female. But it was not her mother, nor a peer, which I at first suspected because the spirit seemed to be standing behind Sheena's shoulder, in my imagination, and then appearing in the peer position.

We went past the 5 minute option to override and Sheena didn't want to quit, so I plowed along. Instead of trying to determine *how* this female spirit was related to Sheena, I decided just to concentrate on the spirit.

I got these following parts correct:

- Long, wavy dark hair when she was younger.

- 1970's diaphanous dress with sleeves.

- Heavy eye makeup and pronounced cheekbones.

- Something wrong with the blood [she had strokes from blood clots].

- I saw her holding Sheena's hands and mumbling something about a loss. So many losses, both physical and emotional.

- I noticed that her nails were painted very well. Even before death, she had a lovely manicure.

- Something was wrong with her hips or legs near the end. She had to walk with a wide stance to keep balance.

- She was trying to belt out "Deck The Halls" and other Christmas songs as loudly as she could.

- She must have partied heavily because there were empty bottles strewn all over the glass coffee table.

- She had so much fun, that I felt I couldn't say too much more in fear I would embarrass Sheena! The word "fun" was an understated euphemism.

Well...Sheena wanted to expand and said that it was a complicated relationship. The spirit-lady was her paternal grandmother, whom she called her soul mate and best friend. I had that it was a female ancestor, but I placed her over the wrong shoulder (right instead of left), and the spirit drifted to the "peer" side of the client. Then again, their relationship was not a typical Grandma – granddaughter relationship. If the spirit had been like a friend, no wonder she felt like Sheena's "peer."

The losses were the loss of oxygen near the end. She also lost her son (Sheena's father). Sheena mentioned that her father never seemed to show up. I told her that I did not feel his presence at all. Because he had died near Christmas, the grandmother began to hate the holiday itself, even though it was her favorite. But in her last two years, she suddenly felt forgiveness and celebrated Christmas with a vengeance, as if to make up for lost time, so Deck Those Halls!

When grandma was alive, she told Sheena that life wasn't worth living if she couldn't have her nails, makeup, and hair done, all the way to the grave. I sensed that her hair was cut short before death like a pixie cut, and dyed reddish. Did she use henna to dye her hair? No, but Sheena confirmed that she dyed it a reddish-purple color to the very end.

Sheena confirmed that her grandmother partied hard, hence the empty bottles all over the place. She loved her men and her motorcycles while alive, and spoke to Sheena like a friend.

I immediately saw various household objects in my mind, and the grandmother was telling Sheena, "Now, a feather duster can be used to get rid of dust from a shelf...but you can also use it to....tee hee!!" And she proceeded to get graphic about feather dusters, cucumbers, and alligator clothespins! How was I going to say this to Sheena? Well, I had to.

Sheena burst out laughing. "That's grandma 110 percent, Russell!! Yes, she would describe the benefits of clothespins for clamps on body parts!"

Oh my.

The things you would not be able to say if standing on platform at church.

Sheena continued, "When granny was alive, she once looked at me and said that if she were as pretty as me, that she'd be the richest escort. I guess that was a compliment?"

I also confirmed to Sheena that her grandmother was telling me about the benefits of having dentures, because you could remove your teeth to....Oh My. Sheena also confirmed this memory.

Sheena asked me to ask her grandma if Auntie Diana and her did well regarding her passing. I told her that I was getting an approving hug that they did the best they could, but then she would launch into this nitpicking and detailing, but in a loving way. Yes, Sheena also confirmed this quirk. She could tell you that she loved you and was appreciative…but you forgot to cross your T's and dot your I's, and you didn't do this right…

In the end, Sheena seemed really pleased about the session. It turned out that we went into 50 minutes, but I wasn't going to charge her for the extra time. I was just enjoying that after the first few minutes of struggle, that the contact with Grandma became stronger and more vivid, thus giving Sheena some closure.

There were lessons to be learned from this phone session.

First, if the client wants one hour, stick with one hour. I could have gone on longer, but I was afraid that I would not last that long.

Second, never profile a spirit. When grandmothers come through, it's easy for the subconscious imagination to want to profile them as sweet, soft-spoken, doing knitting or crocheting. But, all spirits (in flesh or not) are separate spirits with peculiarities that make them colorful. Those details are what count in a reading.

In the end, it felt like Sheena enjoyed the session because she was in a jolly mood when we ended the call.

About 20 minutes after the phone session, I received a text from a cop friend at Valley Traffic Division (VTD). This is what she texted me (I corrected the spelling errors):

"OMG…I meant to text you a funny story. I was having lunch with my friend and your baby picture came up on Facebook. I showed her your picture and she said she knew you from the library and that you predicted something bad was going to happen with LAPD (now known as Rampart Scandal) and you told her she was going to have another boy...all true...she wants your number, needs new advice."

Did the last paragraph sound familiar? Yes? It's from "Chapter 14: 20 Years Later!" This was when I met up with a female officer 20 years later who told me that I predicted 20 years earlier that she would give birth to a third child and that something dangerous was going to happen related to her job, and her husband got fired due to a Department-wide scandal.

What was amusing about this text was that it seemed to come out of left field. I guess it's a small world in LAPD. I didn't know that my current cop friend at VTD in 2023 was also friends with the police officer who used to work Van Nuys Division in the late 1990's when I was a library employee giving her that reading about giving birth to a third child and some danger involving the LAPD.

CHAPTER TWENTY-SIX

How to Conduct a Séance (Mental Mediumship)

Yes, people have asked me how to do it, and while there is no one, right way to do it, I have included points that have seemed to really help.

- Everyone should be in the correct frame of mind. You might have a few skeptics in the circle, and that's OK, but try to have everyone else in the same, proper, respectful attitude. I would not advise approaching this from a thrill-seeking attitude, but rather from an attitude of love and hope.

- No consumption of alcohol or recreational drugs before the séance. It screws with one's energy centers. As a Tarot card reader who once worked at a large party, been there, done that.

- While it helps to have everyone seated in a circle, facing inwards, a table is not necessary. I like a table if only for a place to hold a vase of flowers, a candle, and paper and pens. One séance, we didn't have a table, so I placed a vase of flowers and a candle on the floor in the middle of the sitters.

- Decide who will be the medium. Just one person? Two? Everyone? The medium should do whatever it takes to prepare mentally and spiritually. This is different for every medium. For me, I prefer a short meditation of "Sitting in the Power". If everyone plans to attempt mediumship, everyone can go through the same meditation together, being led by someone, or agree to a certain time limit, say 5 minutes, of meditation/preparation, and everyone can go within and do their own meditation.

- Complete darkness is not necessary. I prefer dim, soft lighting with no background music. At the very least, one candle is fine.

- Raise energy. This can be accomplished by everyone singing the same song/s. Pass around copies of song lyrics before the gathering and perhaps go over the song with everyone beforehand. If you don't like singing, have everyone recite the same thing as one voice, like a chosen prayer or the NSAC's Declaration of Principles. Do you like drumming? Make it a drumming/percussion circle.

As a guideline, you can go in this order, or change the order.

- While seated, say a prayer of protection and guidance, and state the intention for gathering together. Since you'll have a group of individuals who are at different spiritual stages in their lives, a prayer of protection for all involved is a good idea. Hold hands, if you wish, then let go of hands for the meditation.

- Do a meditation/preparation.

- Sing together, and/or recite something together to encourage group cohesiveness.

- Ask if anyone from the spirit realm is here. Stretch out your senses and speak what you sense. It is no good if you stay silent. If you remain silent, you aren't being a medium, but simply listening to spooks. When speaking, you can choose to do the direct or indirect approach.

- This part is where having worked for the police comes in handy. Have a list of questions in your mind ready to ask the spirits such as gender and appearance, career and hobbies when alive, how they died, bodily alterations (tattoos, piercings, amputations, surgeries), favorite memories they shared with the living, artifacts in common with the sitter, personality quirks, favorite foods, favorite places they visited, pets they owned, if they served in the military or police, if they were very religious, etc. Ask if they have a message for someone in the circle.

- If you have not received a satisfactory amount of information for the circle and the energy feels low, sing and/or recite again until you feel the energy go back up.

- When you feel that it's over, say a prayer of thanks. Imagine cords of light extending from your tailbone and the bottoms of your feet reaching way down into the earth below, grounding you.

- Turn on the lights, bring the room "back to normal" and eat something. I love séances that end in either potlucks, or going out to a restaurant. After one particular successful séance, we all ended up going to a goth dance club! Good thing we were already dressed in black clothes.

Tips to Becoming a Better Medium

These tips are in no particular order, but based on my observation. If you think these tips include sitting in the lotus position and meditating for an hour or more, think again! If you are already meditating over an hour in a special position and it's working, keep doing it. I personally don't do this, and popular, unofficial opinion in the police department is, "If it ain't broken, don't fix it."

- Enroll in classes or groups that emphasize public speaking. Listening to spirit is one half of mediumship. The other half is expressing the spiritual information to the living. If you cannot convey messages to the living, you are technically not a medium by simple definition of the word. Also, if doing group work, it helps to be expressive and erudite, otherwise your audience will fall asleep through your dull and boring, "Um, uh, hmm, I guess..." etc.

- Expand your knowledge of the world around you. Try and experience new things. Spirits use your brain-catalog to attempt to convey messages. If a spirit had favorite foods when alive, and the medium only grew up on Americanized spaghetti and meatballs, how will the medium be able to express the complex tastes of Singaporean laksa, Hungarian goulash, or Middle Eastern moutabal? Extra knowledge does not have to be in the occult arts. It can be anything, like traveling, different foods and cultures, different jobs and trades, exposing yourself to unusual names outside of one's primary culture, trying your hand at various arts and crafts, or auditing a college class on an unfamiliar topic.

- Journal your successes.

- When you have reached a certain level of success and feel more comfortable, push yourself further and don't be afraid of making mistakes. For example, I am still working at receiving names. It has happened on occasion where the un-revealed name of the spirit suddenly revealed itself to me and I spoke it out loud to the gasps of the audience and the grin of the sitter's face — and these weren't common names, either. But, it happens very few times, so this is one of my current goals. Maybe a goal might be to receive important numbers and significant dates or times. Or, maybe you want to improve one of your weaker clairs. Of course, you'll get it wrong at first. But then, so do stock market analysts and meteorologists — and they get PAID!

- Focus on being of service to others and on being a vessel of peace and healing, instead of worrying about whether you'll get it wrong, freeze up, etc. If you are fixating on performance anxiety, you are in your ego which will block you.

- Come up with your own codes and classification systems
  with your spirit guides (and your subconscious mind, which
  remembers EVERYTHING). Do spirits send you symbols? Each
  symbol can mean a different thing to different mediums. On the
  flip side of the coin, a particular concept might be represented by
  different symbols to different mediums. "Wedding" might appear
  to one medium as church bells, while the image of church bells
  to another medium might indicate being religious. There is no
  right or wrong answer. This is your own personal dictionary and
  filing system. Keep the bigger picture in mind — finding accurate
  ways to convey information. With my spirit guides, the image
  of an apple always means higher education. The feeling of my
  fingertips tingling means the spirit had diabetes.

- Related to the second point, one overlooked way of improving
  one's mediumship and relationship to the spirits is by living your
  life the way you want your spiritual life to go. It's the reverse
  direction of Art Imitating Life. If you have boundary issues with
  spirits interrupting you while sleeping, take a look at your earthly
  life. Do you have boundary issues with family members? Do they
  not respect your boundaries and personal space? If so, clean up
  your earthly life, set some boundaries, make people observe and
  respect them, and the same will change on the spirit side. Do
  you feel that it might be difficult to hear spirits and sense them?
  Look at your earthly life. Perhaps you might be too introverted
  or too shy. Maybe you isolate yourself a lot and don't enjoy
  meeting and talking with people. Maybe you feel uneasy in social
  situations. If you become more open to being around others (for
  a limited time), you will find that spirits will approach you more

often. Remember, spirits are humans without bodies. So, if you give off the vibe that you don't like to be disturbed, then the spirits will also feel that vibe and avoid you. When in doubt, put yourself in spirit's astral shoes. Would you be more at ease sharing your personal information with someone who is discrete and trustworthy, or with someone who constantly complains loudly, backstabs, and loves to gossip?

It's essentially the Law of Attraction. Be that Law.

- Keep it simple, un-learn things, avoid crutches. This advice is probably more for someone (like myself) who came from another tradition or religion that had a lot of material culture before discovering mediumship (and Spiritualism). For many years, I was involved with neo-shamanism and folk witchcraft. In Spiritualism, mediumship involving contact with Dead People does not require special tools. Now, there are people who come to Spiritualism and bring with them their previous traditions. You might have some Christian Spiritualists who like to wear crosses, refer to the Bible as their holy document, or employ other Christian iconography. A medium who also identifies as a Wiccan might still wear a pentagram pendant. Still, I suggest trying to resist relying on your favorite "lucky stone" in your pocket, or that necklace sporting an amulet or talisman. If you like having these items, keep them and go collect more. Just don't feel that they are necessary for effective mediumship. Remember, you are already a spirit communicating with other spirits (in bodies and without bodies). You are the instrument for contact.

- Humor is GOOD. Humor and good-natured laughter actually

raises vibrations and makes communication much easier. Even when it comes to bringing up the memories of the dearly departed, attitudes don't have to be dour and somber. A platform or public medium who knows how to insert the occasional comic relief can enliven the audience and wake them up. After all, a medium's energy partly relies on the energy levels of the sitters, just like a nightclub comedian performs better with an appreciative and responsive audience. I've also noticed that spirits don't usually dwell on sad memories and tragedies. They can actually be quite funny and bring forth hilarious and accurate information. Since mediumship is a form of healing, and laughter is the best medicine, why not combine both?

Epilogue

Russell's Preamble, to be read by sitters before a reading:

Hello, I am a recently-certified Spiritualist Medium. Before we begin, I should first cover what mediumship is NOT...

It's not "New Age." It's been around forever, cross-culturally. I personally choose to align myself with the National Spiritualist Association of Churches (NSAC.org) and its educational arm, the Morris Pratt Institute (Milwaukee, Wisconsin) due to their history and integrity.

It's not fortune-telling. All mediums are psychic, but not all psychics are mediums. Some mediums can pick up psychic energy around predictions and past/present/future, but this is a separate discipline/practice. I also do not diagnose illnesses and pending deaths due to State laws and I am not a doctor.

It's not palm reading. Palmistry is a fascinating occult art, but has nothing to do with communication from the spirit world to the living.

Astrology, numerology, Tarot cards. I love the Tarot, own over 30 decks, and appreciate the artwork. I will occasionally read the cards, but I'm not that well-versed in numerology and astrology. While these are valid techniques in divination, they are not related to mediumship, nor do I use them in this discipline.

It's not entertainment. In fact, the more I try to do this from a "showing off" or "plain curiosity" intention, the muddier and less-clear the messages seem to be.

It's not therapy. I don't delve into deep emotional problems because I'm not a therapist.

What I Do:

I tune into the spirit world through prayer and meditation. I will bring forth messages and details that I either hear, see, feel, or "just know" from spirit. While I do not and cannot guarantee that a specific spirit will arrive, your intentions and prayers to reach your loved ones are helpful.

Ultimately, I have two goals. First, to illustrate that life is continuous, even beyond death, by bringing forth evidential information. Second, I want to bring healing, closure, relief, and love from the spirit world to the "sitter" (that's you).

Since I am a mental medium, versus a physical medium, objects won't levitate and fly around the room. Ectoplasm won't appear.

What should the sitter do: There are two types of skeptics — the regular skeptic who is willing to suspend Ego, and the cynical skeptic. I am OK working with the former because they keep an open mind and are not trying to block me or disprove me. Some of my first sitters were police officers and police detectives. And, since I'm not making tons of money or going on TV, what have I to prove?

Be an open person. Do not confirm anything unless I ask you, "Does this make sense?" You may answer "yes" or "no" or "I don't understand." If you would like to share more details to flesh out a particular story or anecdote, that's up to you, but don't give me clues or hints so as not to "contaminate" the reading. Never "feed" the medium. Never hold an attitude of desperation. Spirits are attracted to positive energy and love, versus intense sadness. Even in the depths of grieving, it's best to hold a lighter attitude toward the loved-one in spirit,

If something doesn't make sense at first, file it away for later...I have stories about sitters who get an "A-ha" moment much later, or they get information confirmed later, sometimes by someone else. Above all, be patient and respectful since this is sacred/spiritual work. And, every session is always a Big Experiment!

Thank you,
Russell Chan

Cheers to 34 Years
SENIOR ADMIN CLERK
LOS ANGELES POLICE
N1735
Congratulations
on your Retirement
Russell Chan

PEACE OFFICERS ASSOCIATION OF LOS ANGELES
POALA

LAPD

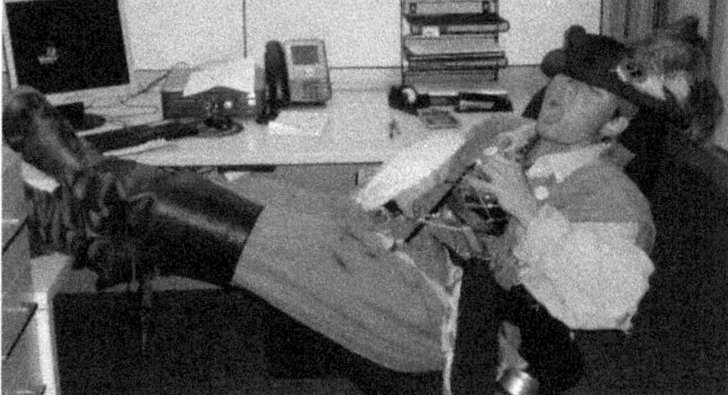

ANGELES POLICE DEPA

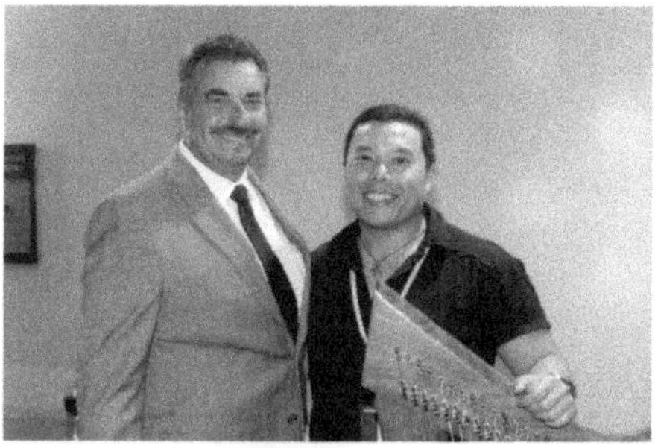

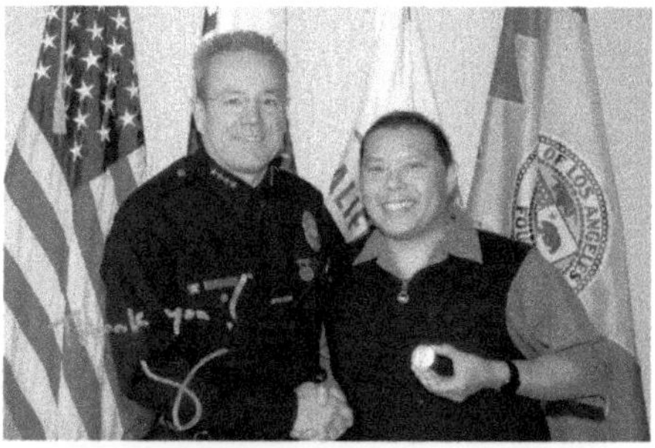

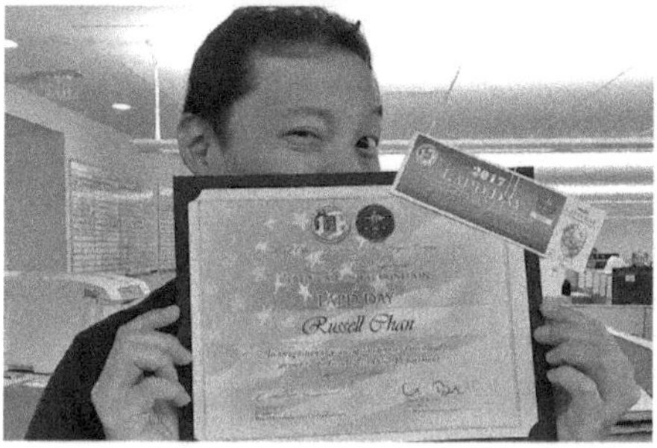
Russell Chan

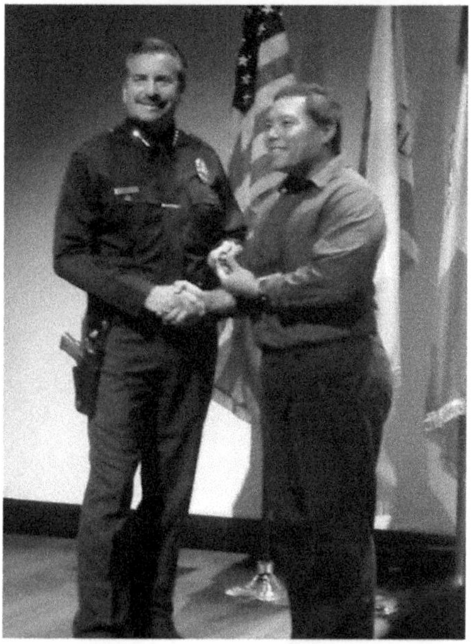

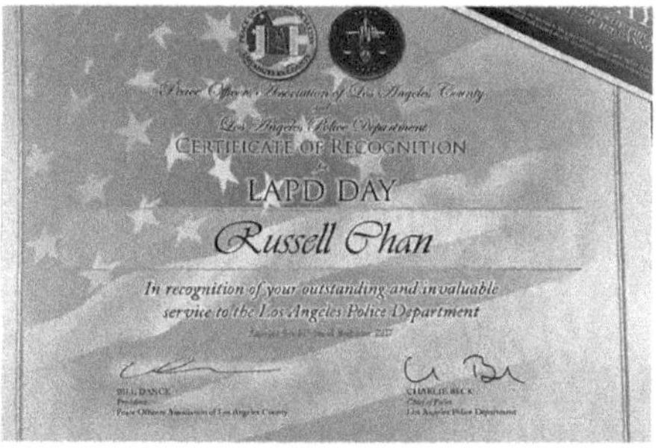
Peace Officers Association of Los Angeles County
Los Angeles Police Department
CERTIFICATE OF RECOGNITION
LAPD DAY
Russell Chan
In recognition of your outstanding and invaluable service to the Los Angeles Police Department

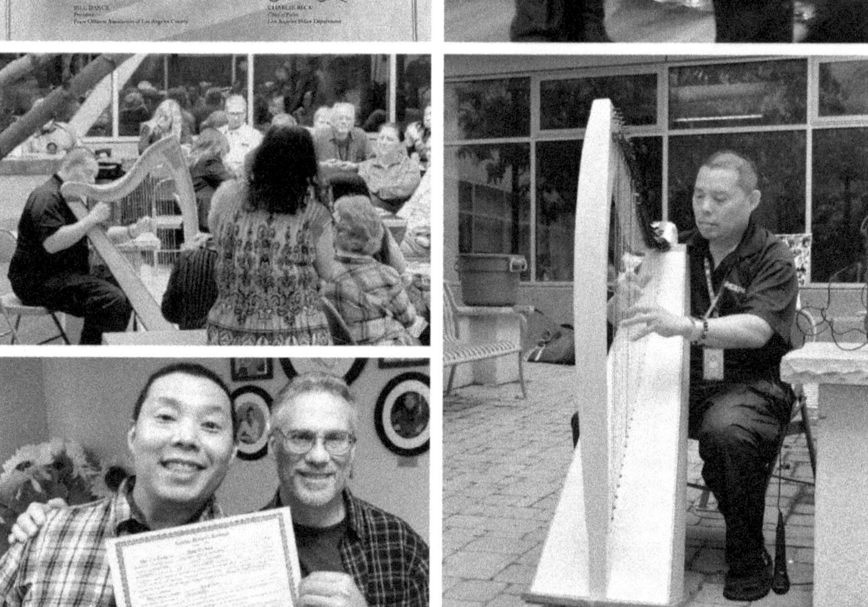

Appendix

Declaration of Principles, from www.NSAC.org

1. We believe in Infinite Intelligence.

2. We believe that the phenomena of Nature, both physical and spiritual, are the expression of Infinite Intelligence.

3. We affirm that a correct understanding of such expression and living in accordance therewith, constitute true religion.

4. We affirm that the existence and personal identity of the individual continue after the change called death.

5. We affirm that communication with the so-called dead is a fact, scientifically proven by the phenomena of Spiritualism.

6. We believe that the highest morality is contained in the Golden Rule: "Do unto others as you would have them do unto you."

7. We affirm the moral responsibility of individuals and that we make our own happiness or unhappiness as we obey or disobey

Nature's physical and spiritual laws.

8. We affirm that the doorway to reformation is never closed against any soul here or hereafter.

9. We affirm that the precepts of Prophecy and Healing are Divine attributes proven through Mediumship.

The 7 Principles of the Spiritualists' National Union (SNU) and the Canadian Spiritualists:[1]

1. The Fatherhood of God

2. The Brotherhood of Man

3. The Communion of Spirits and the Ministry of Angels

4. The Continuous Existence of the Human Soul

5. Personal Responsibility

6. Compensation and Retribution Hereafter for all the Good and Evil Deeds done on Earth

7. Eternal Progress Open to Every Human Soul

---

1. The Spiritualists' National Union, www.snu.org.uk

Acknowledgements

This book would not have been made possible without these people and organizations. I am truly grateful!

To Infinite Intelligence and to my guide, Caelan, who steered me in this direction. Since I used to solo Cessna single-engine planes, I could have been an airline pilot, but noooo...

To my mother, Stella. While we don't always agree on the "outer forms", she showed me what is possible in the world of the physical and the spiritual.

To my late father, Daniel, who, as a child growing up in Singapore, used to create spirit talking boards out of round Chinese dining tables, letters and numbers surrounding the edges, and an overturned tea cup for a planchette, and for his slide presentations of the Monkey God possessing the priest in the Buddhist temple in the late 1960's. If you're wondering why I didn't end up doing sports and being interested in fast cars and firearms, you have my father to thank, even if he did spend the rest of his life as a converted Christian evangelical minister in California.

To my fellow Eagle Scout from Troop 310, high school pal, and the one who watched for my safety in case I ran into homophobic high school bullies, Jeff Sellers. It was Jeff who told me that I should pursue attending a Spiritualist Church and look into becoming a medium. His advice for me and for many other younger generations who look up to him as a father figure has proven to be accurate and true. Coincidentally, when Jeff was a teenager, both his parents were cops in the LAPD.

To Jim Suthers for suggesting the book in the first place, and for his unending support of my adventures. Jim, I love the way you were skeptical when you first met me, then dropped the skepticism after getting a reading from me at church, then further dropped the skepticism after proving to a group that you could do accurate mediumship readings yourself! You are the essence of the skeptic turned reluctant practitioner.

To the sworn and civilian employees of the Los Angeles Police Department — you were my first sitter "guinea pigs" and the primary readers of my email blog, "True Tales From the Platform." I needed to be accurate and transparent with you, first, before getting up on stage in front of the general public.

To the National Spiritualist Association of Churches, the Morris Pratt Institute, and to Spiritualist Church of Revelation in Monrovia, California during the years of 2017-2019, where I earned my credentials. Thank you Robin, Karen, Ernie, Mike, and the late Martin.

Special thanks to the Canadian/Pacific Northwest "contingency." You allowed me to continue practicing while we were in a pandemic lockdown, and have invited me to speak across the border when restrictions lifted. Thanks to Karyl Fay Laird in Seattle, and to the First United Spiritualist Church in Burnaby, British Columbia, Canada.

I made friends and mediumship-practice buddies across the border with the late Lynn Marie Holden, Cindy Mah, Rickie Avitan, Parneet Virdi, Harbinder Pooni, Lynne White, Betty Mathis, and Trudi out on Vancouver Island.

To former officer, friend and knitting buddy, Teru (Lisa) Minohara — thank you for your proofreading, editing, and supplying me the occasional guinea pig.

To Charvonne Carlson and the Church of Peace — A Spiritualist Center, NSAC, my current home church, which happens to only occur online, proving that mediumship still works through computers! Thank you for putting up with my busy schedule in between two countries and beyond. And, here I thought retirement was supposed to be quiet!

To The Green Man Store in Burbank, California — Thank you for patiently booking clients while I was still balancing my schedule with the police department. Thank you to Jill for being one of my phone experiments.

About the author

A native Southern Californian, Russell enjoys traveling, has been to all Seven Continents, has solo piloted single-engine Cessnas in his younger days out of Burbank (BUR) and Whiteman (WHP) Airports, and is an Eagle Scout.

After visiting Wales, he likes to show off
that he can pronounce the town name
of Llanfairpwllgwyngyllgogerychwyrndrobwllllantysiliogogogoch at any moment.

He has a degree in anthropology with an emphasis on cultural.

He appears to enjoy strings: knitting, crocheting, and boasts being the "World's Okayest Celtic Harpist." He has played the Celtic folk-lever harp on a castle stage in County Clare, Ireland (surprising his fellow tour group members along with the castle staff), at weddings, funerals, tea parties, pirate re-enactment events, Spiritualist church services, seasonal holiday events, Celtic pub sessions with other musicians, and police events, but can never play a new song without notice, nor read sheet music proficiently. And, God help his fingering technique.

He now lives in northern Washington State, a ten-minute drive to the Canadian border in case he wants to visit his relatives, both living and dead, visit or speak at a Canadian Spiritualist church, bring back bottles of maple syrup, play harp with the O'Carolan Celtic Ensemble, and to enjoy good ethnic foods.

He is currently a member of Church of Peace—A Spiritualist Center, which is an on-line church with the NSAC.